The Boar Hunt

V.M. Devadas is a Malayalam writer, born in March 1981 in Wadakkancherry, Kerala. He has established himself as a leading voice in contemporary Malayalam fiction, having authored four novels and six collections of short stories. His writing is characterized by a unique stylistic flair, and he often delves into the political and philosophical dimensions of modern life. Devadas's works are known for their unconventional themes, which focus on the hybrid politics of people in our society. He is constantly experimenting with the structure, theme and narration of his works, which has earned him many accolades. He is the recipient of several prestigious awards, including the Kerala Sahitya Akademi Award, Malayala Manorama Novel Carnival Award, Swami Vivekananda Yuva Prathibha Award, O.V. Vijayan Memorial Literary Award and Vaikom Muhammad Basheer Malayala Padana Kendram Award, among others. Currently he is living in Chennai and working as an IT professional.

Prabha Zacharias is a poet and a bilingual translator, born in March 1985 in Kottayam, Kerala. She has published her anthology of poems in Malayalam and has eight full-length books and many short-story translations to her credit. She has completed an M.Phil. in English Literature from the English and Foreign Languages University, Hyderabad, and a Ph.D from the School of Social Sciences, Jawaharlal Nehru University, Delhi. She has worked as an editor at Cambridge University Press, Hyderabad, and Sage Publications, Delhi. A passionate literature teacher, Prabha is currently working as an Assistant Professor at the Department of English and Cultural Studies, CHRIST (Deemed to be University), Delhi.

THE BOAR HUNT

V.M. DEVADAS

translated from the Malayalam by

Prabha Zacharias

hachette INDIA

First published in Malayalam in 2010

This translation first published in 2023 by Hachette India
(Registered name: Hachette Book Publishing India Pvt. Ltd)
An Hachette UK company
www.hachetteindia.com

1

Inside illustration by Harshavardhan Behura
Map illustration by Jit Chowdhury

Certain place names have been used to retain the historicity of the text as far as possible.

Subsequent edition/reprint specifications may be subject to change, including but not limited to cover or inside finishes, paper, text colour and/or colour sections.

ISBN 978-93-93701-79-4

For sale in the Indian Subcontinent only

Hachette Book Publishing India Pvt. Ltd
4th/5th Floors, Corporate Centre,
Plot No. 94, Sector 44, Gurugram 122003, India

Typeset in Faustina 10.5/16.4
by InoSoft Systems, Noida

Printed and bound in India
by Manipal Technologies Limited

MIX
Paper from responsible sources
FSC™ C043100
FSC www.fsc.org

AUTHOR'S DEDICATION

To my wife Nisha and children, Gautham and Gaya.

To my friends, who have been with me in both the tortoise's race and the hare's slumber in my life.

To tango with you tonight?
Oh, what a gamble it would be.
We may as well load five bullets,
instead of one,
spin the chamber and,
pray we both,
survive the aftermath.

MASON FOWLER

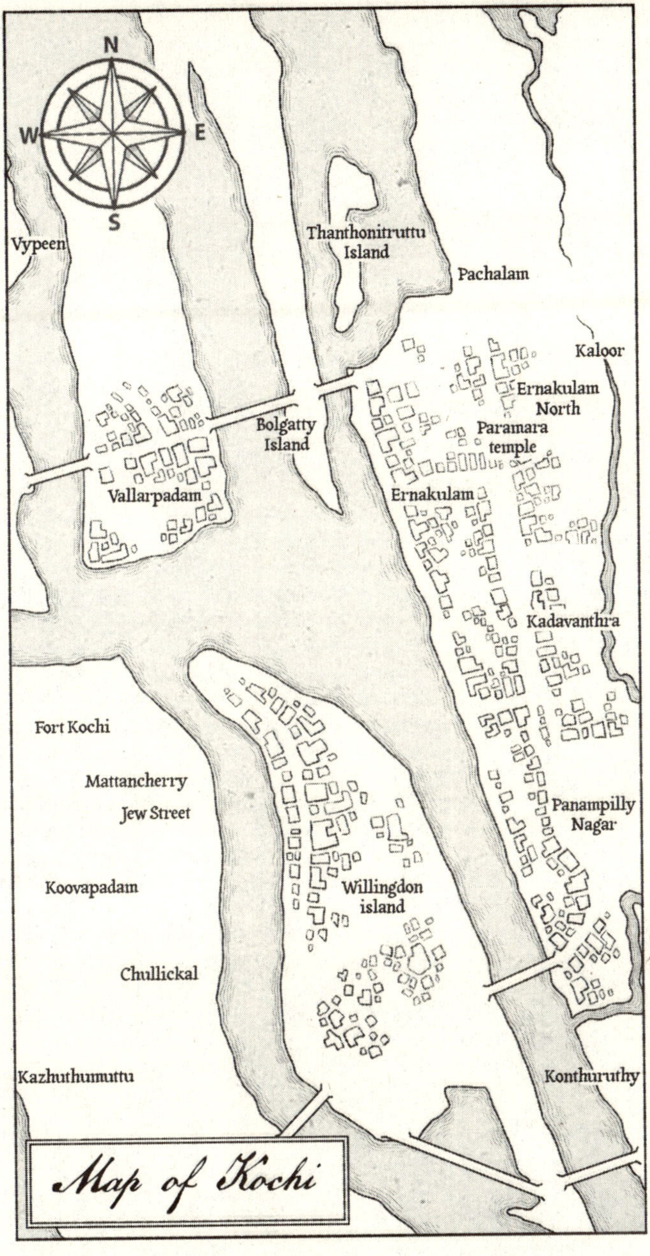

This map is a pictorial representation and not to scale. It is for general illustration only. Neither boundaries nor locations depicted above are accurate or precise and should not be used for reference purposes.

1

The Beginning

Grusha went directly from Kochi airport to Musafir's mental health centre. Her driver parked the rented car outside the hospital gate and waited. Musafir emerged from the building and approached the car with the gait and demeanour of a fifty-year-old. His loose half-sleeved shirt and jeans were faded to the point that they merely held a distant memory of being blue. The grey of the jeans seemed to reflect the colour of his hair. The leather bag in his hand looked like a dismembered body part. One hand strained to clutch the leather bag, while he kept his other hand in his jeans pocket.

Grusha opened the door and stepped out of the car.

Musafir was taken aback. From the look on his face and the question in his eyes, it was evident that he had expected neither the vehicle nor the visitor – a woman, and a foreigner to boot.

Grusha was looking for the beginning of a story. If Raul were to narrate it, it would become the adventurous story of a down-and-out gangster. Getto would insert the language of prophets and lace it with troubling narratives of sexual acts ad nauseam. Unni would include guns, bullets, sex, betrayal and booze, and turn it into a third-rate pulpy movie script. In the hands of retired policeman Bappu, it would end up as a few dry pages in the crime register records at the police station. Given his reticent nature, Dora would leave some scattered elements riddled with mysteries. The Arumukhan twins would not even have a tale to tell. If Satheeshan were the narrator, we would only get a fantasy of a city similar to Gotham without Batman. Lothar would always hide something. Pandam Mustafa might not have anything to narrate until the story was finished.

Sheikh Musafir's Tale... It might be an absurd mosaic, after all. More adventurous than Raul's tale, more romantic than Getto's, more sentimental than Unni's, drabber than Bappu's, more scattered than Dora's, as empty as that of the Arumukhan twins, more fantastic than Satheeshan's, more concealed than Lothar's and even more absent than Mustafa's. Irrespective of all the preconceptions, all of them might narrate a story in the same style.

Since this story is about all of them, why not start with Musafir?

Grusha was aware that Musafir cannot possibly cover the complete story. The people in this tale worked as a gang. Since a gangster cannot stand alone without the gang, their story too would need to be told together. Any other way would be as dangerous as going on a mission with a single bullet in the gun. Grusha would not attempt something like that. For the time being, let us trust her decision.

She tried to soften her accent as much as she could and spoke slowly. 'Good morning, Musafir. I suppose you were not expecting me. The company has sent me to attend to some urgent things. The syndicate must have informed you.'

'I expected either Raul or Arumukhan.'

'You don't have to worry. We are going to meet all of them. Before that, I need to know your gang. That is one important report the company has asked me to prepare.'

Though Grusha invited him to sit in the back seat with her, Musafir sat next to the driver. He smiled at her uncertainly and winked at the driver, easing into the front seat. 'I will show your driver some shortcuts to reach Kochi from Kakkanad,' he said.

They started. From the back seat, Grusha could see inside his leather bag, with its faulty zipper. It contained some books and sheets of white paper with notes scribbled in a language she could not decipher.

'I did not realize you are old... Isn't it tough being a gangster when one is no longer young?'

'"Youth is nimble, age is lame... Youth is wild, and age is tame..."'

'What?'

'Ah! It's a Shakespearean quote.'

That was when Grusha realized that those books in the leather bag were works of Shakespeare.

'Maybe it's good that you are not young...maybe that is why I came to you first. I need to know the story of the gang from the beginning...from Sheikh Musafir.'

Sheikh Musafir – that was how his friends at Calicut Regional Engineering College had addressed him. They could not find a better name for someone who kept quoting Shakespeare all the time. Sheikh Musafir from Kozhippuram used to announce playfully that his hometown was a blend of Kozhikode and Malappuram. His friends would roar with laughter, always looking forward to the delightful Malabar biryani his mother cooked for them.

'We gathered in my room and closed the doors. The seriousness of what we were about to do was evident on our faces. We had a cartoonist amongst us. I suggested taglines for his cartoons, another one wrote them down, and a fourth person gave them the final touches. That was how we protested against the Emergency declared by Indira Priyadarshini. All those who voiced their opinions against the government kept disappearing from all over India. Protest was the need of the hour, and we too formed a group. The posters and notices we made in the room started appearing on the walls around our campus.'

'Were you a Naxalite group?'

'I did not know the name of the short man who used to arrive in a black Willys van carrying notices and instructions. Neither did we find this word in the ideas he brought to us – until the day I was arrested under MISA, the Maintenance of Internal Security Act. I was just a Musafir who used to quote Shakespeare, woo the twinkle-eyed beauties and relish the biryani my umma made in big clay pots as round as the airy dress of a whirling dervish. One day, the police came to our house, asking the same question you asked and smearing with blood the few remaining posters that didn't make it to the walls. We travelled in a police vehicle for the first time, all the while imagining that a black Willys van would overtake the police and the Lilliputian would emerge with weapons and save us from the police. Instead, we lay dazed and soaked in blood under some resting boots, only to be awakened when they threw us out of the police van. We sat on the floor of the police lock-up like flightless baby birds, wounded and bloodied. They asked us about names we had never heard before, showed us blurry photographs and ordered us to identify people. All we knew was a black Willys van – we could not even remember its number – and the short young man who arrived with a bunch of notices. These meagre details were not enough to brand us as traitors. We sat with our heads down, scared and ashamed, hugged each other and cried inside the lock-up that stank of urine. The next day, from overheard conversations, we figured out that they had raided our college campus... It was the day Rajan – do you know of this controversial custodial death of the time? – went missing...

What potions have I drunk of Siren tears,
Distill'd from limbecks foul as hell within,
Applying fears to hopes and hopes to fears,
Still losing when I saw myself to win!

'Then began the torture sessions that left aches that would last a lifetime. We encountered questions whose answers we did not know, beatings that crushed our bodies and the daily naked experience of a lost paradise. Prisons were already crowded. We were locked up in a secret location and branded a dangerous group that required special attention. All we could sense was the deep darkness, the reek of blood mixed with excrement, the screams and groans of tortured bodies. All we could feel was burning hunger. We were beaten twice a day and fed once.

The dented aluminium plates acted both as torture tools and as food plates, sometimes filled with blood and at other times with cold wheat porridge and horse gram mush. No one hoped to escape from that dark dungeon.

'Those with parents and relatives close to the state machinery were let off the hook soon enough. The empty slots were quickly replaced. No one knew the exact number of people that dark room held in captivity. They lay scattered, unable to raise their voices. The only vent for air in that room was a small opening in the wall. We took turns to climb on each other's backs, put our noses close to that opening and inhaled deeply to escape, momentarily, the horrid stench of excrement. We pressed our noses to the hole in the wall and panted like dogs before slowly descending back to the foul miasma. In a way, we resembled noblemen sitting around a hookah waiting for a puff.

'Each time the door opened, we were bombarded with strange questions. None of us there had the strength to resist Jayaram Padikkal, Damodara Marar, Pulikkodan and Kochu Mathew. These police officers even visited our dreams. Our poor tired souls... At the end of each visitation, actual or dream, we used to fall back tired for two or three days, incapable of eating or shitting.

'After our release, we realized that we had been locked up for about four months. It was impossible to measure time inside a dark cell, not knowing day from night, battered black and blue, lost in the madness that swirled in our heads. We deciphered the events in the outside world through conversations between the policemen, the changes in their questions and the variations in the level of violence we endured. The Socialist Party's railway strike led by George Fernandes had ignited in north India. Naxalism had spread towards Andhra and Kerala. Charu Mazumdar, Nagi Reddy and Kunnikkal Narayanan surfaced from their hideouts every now and then. Campuses became the centres of agitation. Anyone who took part in the NGO Teacher's Strike announced by the Marxist party got arrested and later disappeared. Indian jails were overflowing with protesters.

'I was thrown out officially from the college and unofficially from home. Being the head of an orthodox Muslim family, my uppa could not have taken a different decision. He could not let one of the so-called "head-choppers" live in the house. It would mean obstructing their peaceful existence and sabotaging the weddings of my sisters. I went to Wayanad. While my engagement with politics had been half-baked during my college days, in Wayanad, I threw myself into it with my complete consent and knowledge, and started working actively in Kalpetta and Mananthavady.

From fairest creatures we desire increase,
That thereby beauty's rose might never die,
But as the riper should by time decease,
His tender heir might bear his memory.

'We descended the hills with "headless chickens"...a euphemism for guns. The tribal villages and forests became our secret dwelling places. We had to accept help from even the poorest of the poor. I cannot clearly remember those times... I think of myself as a Rip Van Winkle who went into a deep sleep somewhere in the mountains. Enduring the tortures of the prison for four long months had left me half-crazed, so these days we spent as fugitives have vanished from my mind, leaving only a few dream-like scenes in my memory. Children with empty stomachs; men with bent, servile backbones; gloomy women; my travels across the tribal villages; the green stretches; the sleepless nights around the fire; the discussions; the flight; the police whistles...

'By that time, the police had a clear picture of me. We had gathered there secretly to commemorate the eleventh year of the Thalassery–Pulpally action...you know, the attacks on the police stations. There were attempts to unify the work of many standalone groups. We met in a disused spice storehouse. Quite unexpectedly, the police trapped us. It was difficult for the six policemen to tackle us, nine revolutionaries. We scattered and ran in different directions.

'Being the unfortunate one among the lot, I got shot in my left leg while running. I tied the wound up and took a bus from Bathery to reach a friend's place in Calicut. My friend had completed his engineering degree and had secured a job in the government. Since his house was not a safe place, he took me to the home of a vaidyan, a traditional healer, where I stayed in hiding. The medical practitioner was a jovial man. He used to crack jokes and laugh out loud, temporarily alleviating my anxieties. He dug out the bullet and applied medicines to the wound. I hid out with the vaidyan for nine days until I got a message encrypted in a list of medicines. But the police arrested me while I was trying to escape to Mysore. The court decided that my revolutionary activities, including an attempted murder, deserved four years in prison.'

Grusha intervened. 'Musafir, I need to know how you joined the gang and the gang's early history. I think you are elaborating a little too much. Besides, you are not telling me much about this city.'

'This is the only way I can tell my story. You cannot limit a sonnet to the constraints of a haiku. I did not become who I am in a day. You are thoroughly mistaken if you were expecting a gangster like Mikey Cohen or Bumpy Johnson, Bugs Moran or Bugsy Siegel. This is Kochi. Here, if you want to hear a story, you will have to be patient. If my storytelling is not engaging enough, you can talk to the others in your list. But none of them have been in the gang from the beginning.'

'I made a promise to the company that I will send a clear report. I have to abide by it. You know very well how dangerous things have become! That is why I interrupted. I am sorry, Musafir. Please continue the story the way you deem fit.'

Grusha's eyes were fixed on a scaly, red-eyed Chinese rubber dragon hanging from the rearview mirror between Musafir and the driver. She turned her glance back to Musafir. He continued.

'The other prisoners informed me about what I should do once I got out of prison. I planned for new operations from inside the prison and regained my health, even though the pain from the bullet wound persisted. After three years of imprisonment, when I came out on a cold, sleepy night, I immediately moved to my new place of action – Kochi. Little did I know that I would never be able to escape this city. There was a small boat and a boat-keeper waiting for me at the jetty. When I first met Pandrand Albert, he was bored of waiting and kept smoking one cigarette after another. He was just Albert then, without the moniker "Pandrand" or "Twelve". I'll explain that later.'

Like a storyteller at a carnival, Musafir paused to catch his breath, then continued with his story. Grusha realized that he was breathing with difficulty. She tried to picture him as a revolutionary.

'I urgently need to smoke. Can you stop the car for some time?'

Grusha asked the driver to turn the air conditioner off and lower the windows.

'Musafir, like I told you...we do not have time to waste even for a cigarette. I must finish my work here quickly. You can smoke inside the car.'

As the car moved forward, the coils of smoke hit her face and took her back in memory. A group of predominantly Black college students sitting together, singing and smoking. She was one of the only two who did not smoke in that group. She realized that Musafir was not smoking a plain cigarette. She took a deep breath and recognized the familiar scent of marijuana.

'Are you smoking pot?'

'Will you include this as well in your report? Then add this. In colder months, to help with the diseases that riddle his body, Sheikh Musafir smokes up a ganja joint every now and then.'

He massaged both his knees, smiled, closed his eyes and went back to his memories.

Albert took Musafir to an unfamiliar island that night – Vypeen, as he later found out. He lived in a room behind one of the closed shops in a bazaar. In a portion behind Albert's clothes-ironing shop, there were piles of clothes and charcoal. He cleaned up a part of that space for Musafir. The room, with the scent of damp clothes and smoke, reminded him of the prison room he had been locked in during the Emergency. Here was darkness instead of the lush greens of Wayanad, smoke instead of the cold breeze from the hills and the smell of burnt coconut shells instead of the scent of the forest. This room was a localized version of a gas chamber.

The next day, when he met the rebel leader Ayyappan, the first thing Musafir told him was how suffocating the room was. Ayyappan spoke hastily in a distinctly Kochi-accented Malayalam.

'You know, things are a little complicated here with our revolt. There are the ones who died after drinking spurious liquor: many more are still suffering, going blind. Still, the other party, the landlords, is not ready to compromise at all. They had told us they would never let us harvest, even if the crops rot in the water. We harvested the ripe crops from the waterlogged *pokkali* paddy field. That was how the problems began. This year, we did not get to sow. That field is now a shrimp farm. People are in deep trouble; they do not have seeds or land. After the harvest of the *pokkali* field, the police never stopped checking on us. They mercilessly beat up both men and women, who are now half-dead and starving. You cannot go and live in those houses now. We never know when the khaki-wearing maniacs will appear. It is our responsibility to protect you here. Please trust Albert. As long as he is around, nobody will dare to touch you. You will get used to the room in a matter of days...'

Ayyappan left in a rush. Most of the fields were owned by two men, Chandrasenan and Kochagasthy. They had vengefully decided not to cultivate their fields that season and had transformed the paddy fields into a shrimp farm, sinking an entire race of people into the uncertainty of not having anything to eat or drink. Musafir stayed inside the room for three days, curled up, and slept while thinking of an action plan. Albert would go out and collect the clothes to iron early in the morning and get back by the time the sun was up. Then he would heat up the coal and fill his metal iron's firebox. He used to work wearing just a lungi. The heat from the burning coal in the iron made the six-footer's muscular body glisten with sweat. Even though the unbearable heat and the suffocating smoke irked Musafir, he was arriving at some convictions as strong as the flexing muscles in Albert's arms while he ran the giant iron over the crumpled clothes, smoothing them out. On the fourth day, Musafir went with Albert to meet Ayyappan.

'The paddy field is meant for cultivating rice. If they want to run a shrimp farm, they will have to find another place. *Pokkali* paddy fields must flourish here like before and I see only one way to do that. We are going to destroy their shrimp farm. The only doubt I have is whether we should do it discreetly or...'

'Whom should we fear now? It should be done publicly.'

The next day, the shrimp farms were destroyed and the tiny shrimps flowed away with the water. The fields lay orphaned. Musafir hid again in that dark room. Police searched all over the place and beat up anybody and everybody they saw. They reached Albert's shop a day later, looking for Musafir. Without batting an eyelid, Albert told the police that it was his place of work and he had not hidden anybody there. He pushed at a policeman who tried to search inside. The policeman fell. Another policeman helped up his fallen comrade and hit Albert. He hit back. Armed with their batons, the twelve policemen encircled Albert. He picked up the round metal base that shielded the table from the heat of the iron and attacked the twelve policemen all by himself, branding them with the marks from the metal circle. The policemen attacked back. All the while, Musafir peered through a peephole. When he realized that Albert would not be able to hold out much longer, Musafir emerged from the room with his revolver.

'I am Musafir from Wayanad. Who wants to take me?'

Only Musafir knew that the revolver had no bullets. The policemen collected their caps from the floor and withdrew. Ayyappan and others arrived in the evening after hearing about the incident. That was the day Albert became Pandrand Albert. Ayyappan called him that for the first time – he had taken on twelve policemen on his own.

'Ayyappan enquired what my next decision was. He suggested that I find a new place to hide, but I objected. I told him, "You cannot live here in peace so long as I am around. They will calm down for now if they get me. I have decided to surrender. I am not leaving this room. Tomorrow the police will come again. I will surrender then."'

The next noon, Police Constable Bappu came to Albert's shop.

Musafir struggled a bit to recall Bappu's figure for Grusha. Bappu had a rough face, a head glistening with sweat, cropped hair and flaky patches on his scalp, which looked like fish scales. He was more heavily built than Albert, Musafir said.

He threw away a half-smoked cigarette.

When Bappu clanged the handcuffs on the metal iron while walking out with Albert from the ironing room, it gave Musafir a shock. The same shock surfaced on Musafir's face as he narrated the moment to Grusha. He continued his story.

'I went forward with my revolver to surrender. He took hold of it and placed the empty revolver on the ironing table. He came closer. He aimed his fist at my face, but punched Albert on the nose instead. Albert fell down. Bappu then kicked him in the chest. I tried to tell him that I was ready to surrender, but it was in vain. "I am taking you anyway. But is it not disrespectful to leave without properly meeting the guy who beat up twelve policemen?" he asked with contempt.

'Albert lifted himself up from the floor when Bappu slapped him again. He had lost control by then. He attacked back. The two started wrestling and fell out of the shop. For a moment, I contemplated shooting Bappu down, but soon remembered that the revolver had no bullets.

'The struggle of those two bodies entangling, falling, rising again, finally ended. Bappu defeated Pandrand Albert. The tired Albert panted and growled. Bappu took the revolver from the table, put it in his pocket, and handcuffed Albert and me together. We reached Kasaba police station. Bappu never touched me when he came looking for me at the shop – or before and after putting me in the lock-up.

'Two husked coconuts awaited Pandrand Albert. Bappu took the rifle kept in a corner of the station and scraped at the rough surface of the coconuts with the bayonet till they shone like the top of his stubble head. Two constables held Albert's hands tightly across the writer's desk. Bappu approached with the husked coconuts in his hands and crushed Albert's muscles with one from the shoulders down to the arms. I heard Albert crying aloud for the first time. When he fell to the floor, unconscious from the pain, Bappu cracked one coconut open on the floor and sprinkled the coconut water on Albert's face. The policemen held him across the table again. Once the second coconut had done its due diligence, they displayed Albert outside the station without slapping any charges on him. Passers-by moved away, scared to even look at Albert. He lay unconscious by the road the whole night.

'I was the prey set aside for the sub-inspector who came to the station in the evening. The only torture method he seemed to know was to hit one's head against the wall. I felt as if my brain was slowly oozing out of my nose and ears. Darkness filled my eyes, though I could not sense pain after the shock I received to my head. Policemen visited the lock-up whenever they felt like torturing me. Even though I felt as if I was shapeless and spreading all over the lock-up, and despite my memories being faint, I can say without doubt that Constable Bappu did not touch me ever.' He fell silent.

Grusha presumed that Musafir would continue with his story after a short break. He did not. Grusha grew anxious and rubbed her fingers together as the silence extended. The dragon continued to dance between Musafir and the driver. She realized that she was descending into a city-silence where all one could hear was the rumble of vehicles. She wished Musafir would recite a Shakespearean sonnet, if not the story. The silence was unbearable. She even thought of jumping out of the car, for she could not take the silence any more. That was when Musafir asked the driver to stop the car. Grusha had escaped temporarily. Yet she realized that she could not escape from the tales of the city. With every break in the story, she felt that she was moving closer to danger.

Musafir got out of the car. He told her to wait for a minute and crossed the road. He disappeared into a sweet shop across the road. The driver stepped out of the car and emptied a packet of paan masala into his mouth.

Now Grusha was alone inside the car...

No...

There was a Chinese dragon with her, dangling beside the driver's seat.

2

The Dragon

Grusha always fell back on jokes to overcome the terrors that plagued her. Her friend from work in America, Carl Walker, had taught her about this coping mechanism. Carl dealt with his extreme depression by drowning deeper and deeper into internet porn and vulgar jokes. He suggested porn to Grusha too, but she was not interested. To escape from her fears, she edited out her papa from all those scanned family photographs on her laptop. After cutting, erasing and making sure that her father was no longer present in any of the family photographs, she panicked like a gangster who had run out of bullets in the middle of an operation. It was precisely then that Carl sent her an email forward, making fun of her race. It had the picture of a Santa Claus wearing torn clothes and a faded red hat.

A Jewish Santa Claus went out on Christmas Eve for his regular visit. He looked at all the sleeping children, knocked on their doors and asked them, 'Come on...who wants toys at the cheapest rates?'

Initially, Grusha felt intense anger at the racist joke. Later, she laughed out loud. She realized that the joke had helped alleviate her fear – even if only for the moment. It was precisely because of this that she did not complain to the management. Otherwise, Carl Walker would not have lasted in that company another day.

Replying to the email, she sent a picture. A wicked artist had made the image of Christ around a blonde's pubic mound, her golden-brown pubic hair shaped like Christ's beard. The painful jokes turned out to be just what Grusha needed to escape her fears. Carl, too, looked for racist jokes and vulgar images to overcome his depression, and they ended up assisting each other in the game.

Carl's next email used another stereotype to mock his colleague – the idea of a long, oily nose.

Q: *Why did the Jewish beauty chop off her long, oily nose?*
A: *The surgery was cheaper than buying tissue paper to wipe it for a lifetime.*

Grusha replied with a picture of her in a bikini, standing on Miami Beach, her nose smeared in chocolate. After office hours, they walked together through the streets of Dearborn and laughed about the silly things they did during their breaks. Carl smeared some chocolate on Grusha's long nose. She wiped it off with a tissue and smiled. When depression hit him hard, Carl sent another email.

The Italian says, 'I'm tired and thirsty. I must have wine.'

The Russian says, 'I'm tired and thirsty. I must have vodka.'

The Mexican says, 'I'm tired and thirsty. I must have tequila.'

The Jew says, 'I'm tired and thirsty. I must have diabetes.'

Grusha laughed and touched her long nose. Instead of sending a vulgar image as a reply, this time she typed out a long love letter. The minute he received the email, Carl went to Grusha's cubicle with a twinkle in his eyes. That was how Carl Walker became Grusha's lover. That was how, instead of the tedium of their job, love started to overflow in their cubicles in the form of jokes and vulgar images.

Grusha was tired of waiting for Musafir to return from the sweet shop. A procession of people in white clothes passed by, commemorating the death anniversary of Indira Priyadarshini. She remembered seeing a painting by her papa, painted long before she was born, which made fun of the American air force who had tried to interfere in the Indo–Pak war during Indira Priyadarshini's rule.

Grusha's father had been a Russian painter. As a temporary worker in the Soviet Union government's public relations department in Moscow, he had created pictures and posters to justify the communist agenda. He used to finish all the assigned works in a stipulated time with perfect concentration. Painting was not art for him. He painted with the dispassion of a soldier, mechanic or an ice cream vendor. His clothes were always spick and span when he was painting, except for his necktie. His pale neckties were yet another painting tool for him like the brush, the palette knife, the paints or the canvas. He used the tie to clean his brush and his hands. By the time the painting was finished, his tie would have transformed into a kaleidoscope, making it difficult to tell its original colour.

Papa would then present the tie to Grusha. In her toybox, she had many such ties laden with the scent of paint. Her father used to laugh aloud and share many jokes, but the minute he started painting, he would go silent. Everyone was prohibited from his studio while he painted. Even Grusha's mother was afraid to enter the room while he was working. Those restrictions never affected Grusha, though. She would enter the room and keep on irritating her papa, pestering him about when he would give her that tie and asking him innocent questions about the painting. To stop her from disturbing him, he would smear paint on her long nose. She would ignore that and continue to trouble him. Finally, Papa would resort to his last trick. He would stop painting and start to draw a dragon. Grusha would get scared and go away at the sight of the dragon. Once, he had to draw many Chinese dragons to keep the Grusha menace at bay before he could finish his painting. Once it was done, he would pick up all the fearsome dragon images from the floor and tear them up. He would wipe the paint from Grusha's nose, present the colour-smeared tie to her, crack jokes and laugh loudly. Grusha would run to Papa's lap, hug him and rub her nose on his chin to show her affection. Papa would smooth away the strands of brown hair from her face and kiss her on her forehead. Her mother would make fun of her for letting go of her anger so easily.

Grusha's mother was a real kitchen queen. She never joked or played with her daughter. She spent every waking hour in the kitchen, devotedly making tasty dishes. Her empire was the kitchen, just as the studio was Papa's. She detested it if Papa or Grusha entered the kitchen and tasted the half-cooked dishes while she was making them. She would lovingly scold them and tell them that it would all reach the dining table when ready. Like an obedient child, Papa would sit at the table with his hands crossed. However, wanting to irritate her mother, Grusha would go into the kitchen to sniff at the half-cooked dishes and filch some sugar and cheese. Her mother did not have a Chinese dragon in the kitchen to scare her off.

On the day of the fall of the Soviet Union, her papa had drawn a dragon without the intention of scaring her. On his unfinished portrait of Gorbachev, instead of his birthmark on the forehead, he drew a small Chinese dragon.

After the fall of the government, to escape poverty, Grusha's father became a gangster and stopped painting. On cold, dark winter nights, in secret locations inside buildings on dreary streets, he organized the dangerous game of chance called Russian roulette. For a handful of money, groups of hopeless humans flocked to him to try their luck against a revolver with a single bullet in it. They were ready to risk blowing their own heads off. Once his ears grew accustomed to the screams, Grusha's papa stopped cracking jokes and laughing. In his painting studio, now devoid of colour, he spent all his time cleaning his guns and reading an old copy of the Torah. Since there was no longer sufficient food to cook, her mother was also unoccupied in the kitchen.

Grusha never dared ask herself how her father, the one who locked himself up in a room for hours with paint and canvas, could become a hoodlum. On the days of the roulette, she had seen her papa coming back drunk, late at night, and start crying in his painting studio. Once the crying subsided, he would take the Holy Torah and pray for the dead. Standing on his knees, praying and swaying to the rhythm of the chants, an epileptic seizure would get hold of him. Her mother would try to calm him down and hold his hands together but was often thrown to the wall in the face of the demonic force that possessed him. He would be screaming, twitching, biting his lip and frothing at the mouth. Grusha would hide behind her mother's long dress and cry until her father calmed down. He would finally fall asleep on the paint-smeared floor and wake up the next morning, remembering nothing. He would recollect what happened only when he saw the blue marks on her mother's body or when the salt stung his bruised lip or tongue. At breakfast, he would recount the previous night's roulette as if it were a fairy tale. After the seizures during the night, it was as if he had resurrected like a saint.

One day, as they were one person short, Grusha's papa had participated in the bet to keep the game going. But he hadn't even survived the first round. Grusha remembered the day his corpse came home as if it were just yesterday. She had removed the blood-soaked tie from his neck. It was the last souvenir from her papa. Eight months after the fall of the Soviet government, her mother flew to America with a thirteen-year-old Grusha.

It was the time when Russian prostitutes scattered themselves all over the United States and the Middle East, bearing the scent of wild cats in their hair. Her mother soon became a New York whore who bargained for the hours and the number of sexual encounters. From her loins, she printed dollars instead of roubles. Using that money, Grusha finished her graduation in English from a college in Dearborn. It was a college where common people's children studied.

Most of the students were Black. Initially she was not fond of Black people. She loved the white-skinned lot and desired to live like them. But her hair with the scent of wild cats and her speech with its Russian intonation gave her away. She described her painter father as a gangster to her friends. She told them that her papa had been the leader of a Russian gang and since he had a dragon tattoo on his arm, the gang members called him 'The Dragon'. She presented her papa as the winner of thirteen games of Russian roulette. She wove stories where her father's gang members poisoned his drink and when they could not kill him, they shot him and pushed him into a swimming pool.

She was lying.

That was not how her papa died.

That death belonged to the Siberian mystic Rasputin.

Her papa never won thirteen games of roulette.

He was not known as The Dragon.

He was just a painter.

He died a failure in the first round of roulette he ever took part in.

But at the college, among her friends, Grusha, the Russian girl, was the daughter of a gangster infamously known as The Dragon.

The dragon in the car was now still. It distressed Grusha. She reached for her laptop in her bag and started to type an email.

Dear Carl,

I hope you're well. I have reached Kochi and started my work. I am scared for no reason. I wish you would send a Jewish joke to help me out. I know you are in Vegas on your vacation and won't send a joke anytime soon. So I'm sending you a joke my papa told me. ☺

A Jew went to the Soviet embassy and expressed his desire to give up his citizenship and go to a foreign country. The officer at the embassy called him inside.

Officer: Why are you leaving the Soviet Union? What are you lacking here?

Jew: I am afraid of two things.

Officer: Tell me.

Jew: People are speculating about the fall of the Soviet Union. That is my second fear. It is the trend of the times to put all the blame for every wrong turn in the world on the Jews and slaughter them. I am therefore scared for my life. I want to leave the country before something happens to me.

Officer: Are you crazy? This is all fake propaganda. Do you think such a strong communist rule will end? It is not possible, ever.

Jew: Oh! That is my first fear...

With love,

Grusha

3

A Sweet Revenge

Musafir returned with a packet of sweets from the sweet shop. This time, he sat next to Grusha in the back seat. The driver ended his phone call and returned, carrying the scent of paan masala. When the car began to move, the Chinese dragon started to bob about. To distract herself from the toy, Grusha looked out of the window. There were vehicles bending traffic rules and people scrambling round the passing cars. Moving through the bustle of the traffic, Grusha felt that to a keen observer the city offered a musical note with a steady rhythm. A silent procession encroached into a major portion of the road, worsening the situation. Musafir ran his fingers over his greying stubble and turned towards Grusha with a questioning look.

'Do you know what this procession is for?'

'I saw some banners and placards. The driver said it is your ex-prime minister's death anniversary.'

'Oh! Yes. How could I forget that? But I did. I guess the psychiatric medicines are turning me into a rotten vegetable.

If I had not seen this procession, perhaps I wouldn't even remember the death of Indira Priyadarshini.'

Musafir directed the driver to turn the car towards Broadway. Grusha wondered whether things were slipping out of her hands. In the course of the ride, Musafir had subtly and disquietingly transformed into someone different from the man who got into her car at the hospital. She needed to be in control if she was to deal with many more gangsters like him. Musafir placed the oily packet of sweets on top of his bag and continued to narrate his story.

'After a year, in 1983, I was released from prison. I had grown quite distant from the movement, mostly because of my arrest. I was accused of not toeing the party line when I got arrested without consulting the leadership. In prison, none of the political prisoners visited me, nor did I get any secret messages or directions. It was my decision to surrender. I knew what would happen if I did not do that. Instead of Bappu, the entire police force would spread itself all over Puthuvype, Njarakkal, Cherai and Munambam. They would unleash their terror over the already half-dead lives there. That was why I surrendered to Bappu.

'The first thing I did after getting out of prison was to look for Albert. I couldn't find him or his ironing shop anywhere in Vypeen. People had already forgotten the name Pandrand Albert. I found him eventually at Semitherimukku near Ernakulam North. He was running a makeshift flower shop next to his brother Simon's watch-repair shop. Behind the funeral wreaths displayed in front of the shop, I saw a thin stick figure of a person trying to smile. It was Albert – but not the Pandrand Albert I knew. Two coconuts and numerous metal-encrusted boots had transformed him from Pandrand Albert into this. He was happy to see me. When he smiled from ear to ear, he resembled a corpse. He laughed and laughed, and then he coughed, breathed with great difficulty, spat out thick phlegm, rubbed his chest and cursed, "Even dead, his body will keep burning."

'I understood that the curses were for Constable Bappu. I saw Albert struggling to lift a garland of flowers – the Albert who once toyed around with a metal iron that weighed around five kilograms. I left. Pandrand Albert died in my mind that day, years before Albert and his brother died for real in a bomb blast. I am glad his life ended like that. He would have suffered living a useless life...'

'Oh, so Albert is no more?'

'No. Do not include his name in the list you are sending to the company. You do not need the dead, all right? You only need those who are willing to die.'

Grusha shrugged her shoulders, reached for a tissue paper and dabbed her nose. Soon the tissue paper turned as oily as Musafir's sweet packet. Musafir kept staring at the packet.

Musafir was at a teashop in Kadavanthra, eating a jalebi, on 31 October 1984, when he heard about Indira Priyadarshini getting shot. He stopped eating, looked at the stack of sweets in the glass case and asked the shopkeeper to pack all the jalebis he had. There were thirty-one jalebis. Holding the oily packet in his left hand, Musafir rode his bicycle with just his right hand until he reached Broadway. His bicycle swayed this way and that, resembling an angry fist moving up and down to the rhythm of the slogans.

Musafir had a Sikh friend in Broadway, Ernakulam. His family had been traders for two generations. His shop was stocked with sacks of raisins, pepper, cinnamon, cloves, cardamom, mace and nutmeg. During Musafir's long conversations with his friend at the shop counter, his four-year-old daughter would sit and munch on raisins. She was a wheat-toned, green-eyed, naughty little girl. Her father would look at her and tease her by calling her 'rotten-toothed'. She would start crying. To soothe her, Musafir would pretend to scold her father. His friend would act sad. Musafir would then take her riding in his cycle till she was back to her cheerful self. Back at the shop, she would grab a handful of raisins and give them to Musafir as a reward for standing up for her. Musafir would jokingly tell her that it was the first time he got a fee for being a gangster.

The bicycle ride to his friend's shop was strenuous. He climbed off the cycle, panting, and called, 'Neela Tharakame!' (Blue Star – the code name of the Indian military action at the Golden Temple against Sikh extremist leader Bhindranwale – an odd nickname, but this was Kochi, and her parents knew that their friend Musafir was eccentric). The girl came running out of the shop. He gave her the jalebi packet. Musafir's friend looked on, his eyes brimming with wonder. Musafir shouted, 'Eat this as a means of healing the harm inflicted upon your clan.' He laughed. His friend's face lit up. His daughter put the packet on top of the sack of raisins, opened it and started counting the oily, syrupy jalebis with her tiny fingers. Meanwhile, in Delhi, surgeons were extracting thirty-one bullets from Indira Priyadarshini's body. The girl stopped counting, took a jalebi and tasted it, spilling oily red syrup from the corners of her mouth. Musafir looked at her and called out, 'Neela Tharakame'.

The news bulletin ended. Sad memorial music started playing on the radio. His Sikh friend closed the shop in a hurry.

On 31 October every year, Musafir reached the shop without fail. His friend succumbed to a heart attack. His 'Neela Tharakame' grew up to become Neelam Kaur, although Musafir continued to call her the Blue Star.

The car entered Broadway. Grusha saw the congested street and laughed to herself. The irony of it being called 'Broadway' was too apparent to be overlooked. Musafir tapped the driver's shoulder and directed him to stop in front of a spice shop, took the packet of sweets and got out of the car. He called out loudly, 'Neela Tharakame!' A tall, hefty young woman came out with a little girl holding on to her hand. Musafir gave the packet to the little girl. Neelam Kaur's husband came out and whispered something in Musafir's ears. Musafir walked back to the car swiftly, got in and slammed the door shut. Grusha noticed him sweating profusely, his lips trembling, his eyes closed. The girl ran towards the car with a handful of raisins for Musafir and lowered her eyes when she saw the car speeding away.

Musafir sat back, struggling to breathe. Grusha gathered that something unexpected had happened, but she waited for Musafir to reveal it. She turned towards the Chinese dragon. Worried about the memories of her father crowding her thoughts again, she breathed a sigh of relief when Musafir broke his silence.

'Where are we headed with these godforsaken games the company plays? Who knows? It is going to destroy us all. You might have to make changes in your list of names for the roulette. The gang is getting ready for a big change.'

Realizing that Grusha had not understood, he added, 'Raul is dead.'

4

The Gangs

The gangs of Kochi were not made in a day. As Kochi's role as a major centre of commerce declined, the gangs thrived. In the beginning were the first-generation smugglers, unemployed young men and the fishermen who abandoned their trade and joined these groups, huddling on the beaches and lakefronts, rowing their small boats to the big ships anchored in the sea, in search of things to sell. They escaped the watchful eyes of the authorities, and smuggled gold, foreign liquor, cigarettes, clothes and electronic gadgets at night. The work they did was illegal. Yet they held on to their ethics. Betrayers met with death. During raids, they guarded their secrets, suffered beatings and took turns to stay in prison to protect their sources. As these gangs prospered, other groups emerged without any ethics at all. Their modus operandi was different. They arrived with their boats, stole parts of anchored ships, propellers of smaller ships and copper wires from the harbour's electric lines, robbed ship workers and made away with stuff from goods carriers.

Over time, as security measures strengthened by the shore and in the sea, these petty thieves grew lazy and started betting in their spare time. This evolved into another business – of running bets. Their favourite activity was something they called 'the cotton game'. They ran bets over the numbers printed on the cargo boxes carrying cotton. The small kiosks next to these docks became betting stations. There were disputes, and then there were mediators to deal with disputes.

Once Kochi became a tourist destination, the second generation of gangs surfaced. All those who smuggled gold and cigarettes started to sell marijuana and heroin. Ethics had no place in the way they conducted their business. Violence and retribution became commonplace.

Kochi was changing.

The cotton game gave way to single-digit lotteries.

All those who smuggled drugs started trading in arms...

Poor prostitutes became escort service girls.

Smugglers, betrayers, thugs, pimps.

By the time industries began flourishing in Kochi, the third generation of gangsters arrived on the scene. Goons and prostitutes feared the police. The police obeyed the industrialists. Politicians threaded them all in an invisible string of fear and commerce, integrating the industrialists, goons, police, prostitutes and the real estate guys. Eventually, different groups formed, fought, split and reconciled into various combinations.

In the late eighties, Musafir started to work with a gang called Mochanam, meaning liberation, a group of people who had strayed from the extreme left organizations. They took a strong stand against the trouble-making goons who disrupted the organized operations of the gangs. Through warnings, discussions and protests, they tried to resolve issues among the gangs. Both the police and the goons kept looking out for Musafir and his friends.

Once, Musafir was attacked when he went for a discussion at AKG Colony with six others from Mochanam. The discussion ended peacefully, and the other members left. Musafir continued his discussion with the gang leader and then went to meet a friend who lived nearby. On his way back, a man who had been part of the peaceful discussion earlier stopped Musafir and kicked him to the ground. The man took out a dagger he had hidden under his shirt. Musafir tried to run, but the knife gouged out a piece of flesh from his thigh. Another strike made a deep gash on his leg. Caught unawares by the attack, Musafir cried aloud, and his friend came running. The young attacker took off his shirt, wrapped the knife in it and ran away. The city of Kochi later named him 'Pandam' Mustafa, giving him the epithet of 'goldsmith'. Pandam is an ambiguous term – on the one hand, it is a word used to refer to gold jewellery that is commonly pawned in exchange for money. Another meaning refers to your internal organs when they spill out after a knife attack to your belly.

Musafir had to be admitted to a hospital. Infection spread from his thigh. He became crazed with the ceaseless pain. Albert visited Musafir at the hospital every now and then, even though he was in a more pathetic state than Musafir. While Musafir shouted out Shakespearean sonnets deliriously, Albert coughed and coughed and cursed Bappu. When Musafir's screams began bothering other patients, doctors suggested shifting him to the mental asylum at Kumudagiri, Kakkanad. Albert and Simon took him to Kumudagiri. His madness played hide-and-seek with him. He kept to himself in his cell. In the throes of madness, he recited sonnets, and when he was better, he wrote poems. He came out of the hospital after four months to face a warrant charging him with attacking six people, including a young man named Mustafa at AKG Colony. After the trial, Musafir was imprisoned once more. That was where he met Shashidharan again.

They had met for the first time at an inter-university talent festival in college.

It was the late seventies. The Indira era had ended. Vietnam had ended. The Spring Thunder – the peak of the Naxalbari movement – had begun to wither under the heat of state repression. The campus was as high as Musafir. A group of people emerged, sporting identity crises, and drank cheap arrack, smoked up and whored around. They gathered around, discussed Camus, Kafka and Sartre, and recited the poems of Gibran and Shelley. There were writers' camps and street plays. Campuses revolted and many students were thrown out.

Writers like Mukundan, Chullikkadu, Kadammanitta, Backer and John Abraham lazed around, listening to the bells of Haridwar, smelled the burnt corpses of Black children and drowned in romanticism.

The rebel students populated the party offices, cinema halls and booze shops. The college campus was at its politicized best. They split into right wing and left, created martyrs, protested and celebrated memorials.

Later, Musafir dropped out of his engineering degree, but Shashidharan completed his graduation. Then he worked in a newspaper for a year and a half before reaching Maharajas

College, Kochi, for his postgraduation. Campus transformed again when money started to spill out. In the place of martyrs came the victims of ragging. Cricket commentaries from pocket radios filled the alleyways where poetry was heard earlier. Kapil Dev, Sunil Gavaskar and Michael Jackson became the poster boys. People banged their heads to the tune of Pink Floyd. Girls planted shy wet kisses on the pictures of Gavaskar and Venu Nagavally.

Shashidharan was imprisoned for a murder attempt. He had been dismissed from university. He shared stories about dishonest politics and the growing gangs of Kochi with his fellow prisoner, Musafir, who was there after the AKG Colony incident, and talked about the group that he planned to start as soon as he was out of jail.

Musafir joined Shashidharan's group, a motley collection of misfits from the left groups, who had no college or home to turn to, as soon as he was out. Struggling to survive amongst the goons, politicians and police in Kochi, they evolved into a parallel gang, largely anonymous. Initially, Shashidharan's gang contacted those who needed their help, created watertight deals they could not refuse and appeared out of the dark to attack the notorious goons of Kochi. They started planning and executing their missions and eventually became powerful, spreading their tentacles of fear across the city. People started looking out for them. Their sense of urgency and justice earned them the trust of people. Musafir's rented house at Kadavanthra was their hangout. When Musafir was hospitalized during his bouts of madness, they met at Albert's flower shop or Simon's watch-repair shop. If Shashidharan was the king of the gang, Musafir was his most trusted minister. Shashidharan at times addressed him playfully as 'wazir', the king's minister. Shashidharan was the leader, but Musafir was the advisor with the power to control everyone in the gang.

Despite the terror his gang was in the city, Musafir was the calmest inmate in the mental asylum. He seldom slept but wrote poems and recited them loudly from his cell. Shashidharan named Musafir's collection of poems *Moonshine* and had them published. The book had a cover image of a wolf howling at a full moon.

On the night after its publication, Shashidharan was stabbed to death on Veekshanam Road. His corpse lay there until morning. Musafir saw the body and started to howl. After Shashidharan's cremation, Musafir went home and burned all the copies of *Moonshine*. He screamed when the fire from the books licked his clothes. Gang members rushed in and stopped the fire. They took him to the mental asylum in Kakkanad. Musafir received his first shock treatment on the day the leadership changed in the gang. He squirmed in his bed like a wave and saw himself as a dervish spiralling to the tune of loud music. When the music stopped, the dervish fell down to the ground with frothy spume at the corners of his mouth.

The gang tried to make Musafir their leader after Shashidharan was murdered, but they soon realized that an unstable Musafir, who spent half his time in an asylum, was not fit to be a leader. However, all of them continued to obey his orders. He designed their moves. Whenever he had disagreements with the leader or was doubtful of the trustworthiness of a gang member, he shouted at the top of his voice. He only took part in operations carried out at night. For Sheikh Musafir, one rule was inviolable: he would not see the face of the victim or the event itself. After each attack, he returned home drunk and recited poems. The gangsters took him to the asylum during his bouts of madness and brought him back when he recovered.

After another twelve years, in the late nineties, Raul became the gang leader when all those who were older in age and higher in rank to him died in an operation at Eloor and in police custody. He was a medical student before he joined the gang. While he was not extremely bright, he was an above-average student. His professor's daughter, a classmate at the medical college, fell in love with the fair and handsome, six-foot-tall Raul. He fell madly in love with her. When word of their love affair got out, Raul started to fail in his exams. His reports were perfect in practical exams, yet he failed. Teachers did not sign his dutifully submitted work records. Raul couldn't go beyond the third year. The gentle professor smiled the day Raul was dismissed from the college on fake charges of stealing and selling drugs from the college laboratory.

By the time he was released from prison, the professor's daughter had reached her residency. Raul entered the medical college as a medical representative with the help of some of his old classmates. He became renowned in his company with his clever marketing methods. He visited the professor's daughter at the hospital regularly with his suitcase full of drugs. In deserted hospital corners, they continued their romance amidst cries, broken limbs and death. At times, he playfully took her stethoscope and wore it like a child who had found his lost toy. She would then tease him by calling him a 'fake doctor'.

He would pretend to be hurt and remove the stethoscope. The professor intervened again in their hospital-scented love affair. Raul was arrested again for selling fake medicines. Bappu beat him to a pulp inside the lock-up while reminding him to forget that girl. The professor got his daughter forcibly married while Raul was in prison. By the time Raul was out, she had started higher studies in forensic surgery.

Raul met Musafir through a fellow ex-inmate. Musafir still remembered the day. He had just finished writing a poem and was rolling a joint. He removed the tobacco from the cigarette, mixed it with weed, refilled the tube of cigarette paper, took the refill out of the pen in his pocket to tamp it down and moistened the plug wrap paper with his spit. He had noticed the presence of the young man in the room, but he paid attention to him only after lighting the joint. He took two drags and asked Raul to read the poem. The man accompanying Raul winked at him and suggested he play along. Raul remembered the medicine-scented girl while he read that love poem.

Musafir placed Raul's first weapon in his hands, effectively erasing that memory.

The professor in Raul's love story had retired and was dreaming about his son going to the United States for higher studies and his daughter working as the forensic surgeon for the government – when Raul struck. A young man who was supposed to take off for the United States in two days was attacked in a bar while he was giving his friends a treat. Raul was later hospitalized and complained that it was the young man who had attacked him. The old professor came to the hospital pleading for mercy. With a smile, Raul recited an anatomy answer, titled 'Capsule and Ligaments', he had memorized. He drew the picture of the adductor canal with his finger in the air. The professor left, bearing the guilt of a doctor whose mistake had led to the death of a patient. Two weeks later, his wife was suspended from government service for taking a bribe from a patient. According to the court documents, the patient's name was listed as Raul Sebastian.

Raul was constantly in the grip of ailments. In his encounter with Bappu, he broke his nose and subsequently suffered from bouts of sinusitis. He was often riddled with persistent colds and migraines. When his tonsillitis became severe, he struggled to drink water. To get some relief from his tooth cavities, he kept chewing on raw tobacco. Musafir used to joke that none of the organs in Raul's head worked properly except for his brain. Whenever the migraine intensified, a blue vein used to bulge on the right side of his forehead, looking like an infant snake on his pale face. He felt each beat of that vein like a metal hammer in his head. Doctors prescribed surgery for him, after which he was supposed to rest for two months without moving his head. Not wanting to keep himself away from the activities of the gang for so long, he kept postponing the surgery. He believed in the adage, 'You retire from the gang when you die.' The nasal spray he used to prevent sinusitis kicked up a dry desert inside his nose. It bled occasionally. His white handkerchiefs resembled a sanitary napkin on the days of medium flow. When his migraine got severe, he put his finger down his throat and vomited. When he started to vomit, the pornographic image of a drug-scented girl fellating another man appeared in his mind. Once he had removed all the poison from that small snake residing in his forehead, he would sleep, exhausted. He used to see strange dreams in those sleep cycles. The next day, he told Musafir about all his nightmares.

In a recurring dream, a giant lizard would be pulling an iceberg. The lizard, its chain and the iceberg would move slowly. As the iceberg melted, the lizard and its chain shrank. When the lizard had shrunk enough to resemble an ordinary house lizard, he would wake up. Whenever he spoke about this strange dream, Musafir would respond in two different ways, depending on his own state of mind.

'All these are your migraine dreams. There are many studies about such strange visions. There is no need to take it seriously.' This was the 'sane' Musafir.

Once, Raul told the 'mad' Musafir about his dream while he was in the mental asylum. Musafir closed *The Tempest* and talked to him as if he was in a Shakespearean play.

'That iceberg is our gang. The chain signifies our unity. The lizard represents the gang leaders over the years. The vision talks about the weakening of the gang. It might be a sign telling us about an upcoming danger. The unjust sun is getting warmer and warmer. The dream is reminding you about the life of the iceberg driven by a lizard. All the leaders of the gang from Shashidharan onwards have had this dream.'

After this analysis by Musafir, Raul became more careful. He returned to the gang even more energized after each migraine attack and performed more operations with utmost care. Musafir's mad haikus contained it all.

A leader's lone attempt
To relieve headaches of
An uprooted gang.

Their gang remained a strong group until Musafir was admitted to the hospital three months earlier. The problems in their gang started when Raul's aunt, Sister Rita, decided to give up her sacred vows. After school, Sister Rita had entered a convent and worked in India and abroad for many years as a missionary. She started having some issues with the church. When she realized that it would be difficult for her to go along with the rules of the church, she started getting involved in social service activities outside the church. The church warned the rebel nun. Eventually, she decided to give up her habit. The media celebrated her renouncement and churned out news for and against her decision. Some leftist organizations that were waiting for a chance to jump at the church joined the bandwagon, and the issue spread like wildfire. In a Christian newspaper's daily cartoon, Rita was mocked as the naked Eve and the leftist organizations as Satan. Raul destroyed the newspaper's office. The paper owners hired Pandam Mustafa so that they could be the first to print the news of Raul's death.

Mustafa knew very well that getting Raul would be difficult. Mustafa and his friends were waiting for a chance when they came to know that Getto, a north-eastern member of Raul's gang, was not on good terms with him. Mustafa reached out to Getto through Unni, who had once been part of the gang and was now a real estate dealer. Getto knew the secrets of the gang and betrayed Raul. While Raul was travelling from Mulanthuruthy to Kochi on a bike, Mustafa and one of his gang members attacked him. Slashed on his left arm, Raul fell to the ground but quickly stood up and drew his gun. The attackers ran off into the darkness. Though he didn't see Mustafa clearly, Raul recognized his companion. He got his wound sewn at the Medical Trust Hospital and sped off to Pullepady on his bike. Pandam Mustafa's companion was found dead near North railway station later.

Raul went into hiding in a house at Nayarambalam. The congested room made him restless. Ants grew aplenty in that damp room after the rains. Raul was afraid of ants. It was neither the shape nor the sting of ants of which he was wary. It was the discomfiting vision of ants carrying a lizard that had died dragging an iceberg for too long. Ants were omens for him. Instead of attacking him directly, ants would enter his space like Trojan warriors and attack his bed, pillow and blanket. Before he shifted to the college hostel, before he was expelled from the college, before he was imprisoned, when he was in hiding – ants would arrive two or three days before every major shift in his life, and make his bed and pillow their abode. Disturbed at the loss of his habitat, he would stomp on the ants. He would clean his mattress relentlessly, but the ants would return with a vengeance.

Ants infested that house. Being cooped up inside had become unbearable for him. To escape his boredom, Raul made elaborate plans to attack those tiny ants. A piece of dosa or a bit of bread with some jam became magical traps to attract large groups of ants. Raul would pretend to be Gulliver and sleep while the Lilliputian ants tried to carry the food away. He would order the scrambling ants to stop. He would then jump up and crush them all together with a piece of paper or cloth. When he was done with them, the space would resemble a battlefield. He would still be killing those half-dead ones. The smart ones among the ants would hide inside the cracks in the walls. Raul would take the gum he was chewing on, part it into sections and use it to seal all the cracks shut. He would create tiny gum Guantanamos around the switchboard, the corners of the wall and the cracks in the floor.

Raul was transforming himself into an ant. To avoid the visits of his gang members bearing food, he changed his eating habits and started to survive on bread, raisins, biscuits and dates. One day, to avoid the boredom inside, he went out in the rain. The rain showered down on him with kindness. He returned all drenched and lay down. In his sleep, he started sneezing. His fever heightened. His stomach gave up after all the mouldy bread and raisins he had eaten. The severe gastritis made him feel like a balloon, a heavy weight hanging from his chest to his underbelly. The irritation and pain increased as if he was impregnated with a huge lump of meat. He started to fear that he might die from fever and indigestion. Even though he could barely stand, he limped to the kitchen to boil some water. There was only one matchstick left in the damp matchbox he found in the kitchen. He uttered what was probably the sincerest prayer of his life. Luckily, it worked.

While drinking the warm water, Raul felt the existence of each internal organ he had learned about in his anatomy class. He breathed with difficulty. The warm water had started to work inside his body. His body was divided into two at his navel. When the diarrhoea and vomiting started, his body became a physics experiment in which conjoined hollow semi-spheres stayed motionless while horses tried to pull them from both ends. He ran from the washbasin to the toilet constantly. Soon, he was too dehydrated to walk. His bed became the site of his vomiting and diarrhoea. The pressure of his strained breath caused his nose to bleed. He was found frozen and dead on that green mattress soiled with his vomit and shit. The scared ants came down from the cracks in the walls and covered Raul. Making sure that there were no more sneezes and coughs left in him, the ants marched like soldiers into his bloodstained nostrils.

It was the ants who first certified Raul's death. Only later did his body lie in wait at the post-mortem table for a drug-scented girl to dissect and confirm. She reached the hospital after the police intimation and stood shocked when they removed the cloth that covered his body. He lay naked in front of her. She caressed his half-shut eyes, his swollen cheeks and his vomit-encrusted beard without wearing her surgical gloves. While she ran the blade through his frozen body, they went back to their old classroom, they giggled, held hands and roamed around. They kissed behind closed doors. After the autopsy, she wanted to hide like an ant inside his body and sew it shut. Raul's body was removed from the post-mortem table. When it was carried through the corridor, a dead lizard fell from the ceiling onto the corpse.

5

The Sixth Bullet

Grusha opened her laptop and sent a one-line email. She repeated what Musafir had told her.

'Raul is dead.'

She then looked towards Musafir, who was still in shock.

Transfixed on the Chinese dragon figurine, his eyes were watery. Grusha looked away towards the city. When she was bored with the cityscape, she asked Musafir, 'Where shall we go now?'

'Don't you need to rest? I am going to see Raul. He will be tired waiting for me.'

'I am not going to the hotel for now. I need to send a detailed report. I am coming with you, if that is okay.'

'I don't mind, although he does not like meeting strangers. But now he cannot do anything about it, right? So that is fine.'

Musafir tried to feign a smile. Grusha too tried to smile but failed.

After the post-mortem and other police procedures, Raul's body was brought to Musafir's house at Kadavanthra. Raul lay on a white bed sheet, calm like someone who had just finished all his important responsibilities. A few ants wandered around on the bed sheet as if they were lost. A small crowd had gathered near Musafir's house. Two policemen stood a little farther off, observing the crowd. Grusha's car arrived in front of the house and parted the crowd into two on its way. She opened the door and helped Musafir get out. He felt like a really old man. He grabbed his leather bag, held on to Grusha with his other hand and entered the house. Everybody's attention diverted from Raul's body towards Musafir and Grusha. Sister Rita sat near the corpse, reciting prayers from a book she held in her hands. Arumukhan sat next to her and whimpered to the rhythm of the prayer. When he saw Musafir, he went to him, put his hands on Musafir's shoulders and wept uncontrollably. Musafir took Arumukhan's hands in his own, pointed at a wound on his left hand and said, 'Look, the one who is lying there dead once tried to kill you for your mistake. He doesn't like all this. Please stop crying.'

Arumukhan stopped crying, like a machine operating on command. He wiped his tears with his bruised hand. Musafir touched Arumukhan on his shoulder and asked, 'Where is Satheeshan? Is he not around?'

Hearing Musafir's voice, Satheeshan came out from a room inside the house. Musafir pointed towards Grusha and said, 'This is Grusha. The company has sent her to check if everything is in order. Things should go on as we have planned.' He continued, turning towards Grusha, 'While I was away in the hospital and

Raul was away taking care of me, he managed everything here. You can approach Satheeshan for anything now.'

Musafir went inside his room and closed the door, avoiding looking at Raul's dead body even by accident. Raul lay there, waiting for Musafir's attention just like his first day in the gang. Musafir grabbed a packet of weed from his table. Though it was three months old, he rolled a joint and smoked up. Then he opened his door and came out with the half-smoked joint. He looked at Arumukhan, who immediately took a chair and placed it near Raul's head. Musafir sat there, stretched his legs out, took a drag and then became still. He looked at the corpse without blinking, and his eyes started watering. Satheeshan approached him and touched his shoulder. He put out the cigarette by crushing it on the arm of the chair, took Satheeshan's hand and pressed it against his face. Satheeshan helped him up and led him towards the inner room.

Once the door was closed, he explained the circumstances of Raul's death to Musafir. Grusha knocked on the door, interrupting them. They came out of the room.

'Musafir, I am leaving. I need to go to the hotel and rest for a bit. I will have to convey the incidents here to the company as well. Since Raul is dead, I need to prepare a list of alternatives. Perhaps I will meet retired police ASI Bappu in the evening. If it is not convenient for him, I will postpone the meeting to tomorrow. I think he can give more details about Kochi and about Mustafa's gang. When is the funeral?'

'In the evening.'

'I will try to return before that.'

Before leaving the room, Grusha looked at Raul's face one last time. She hoped that he would kick the white sheet away, take out a hidden gun from his waist and scream at her, asking her to stay. She entered the car. It moved and disappeared into the crowd. A police constable who stood a little farther away took a piece of paper from his pocket and jotted down the number of the car.

Musafir lit a second joint in his room and coughed vigorously as the ganja smoke entered his lungs. Arumukhan knocked on the half-closed door. He stuck his head into the room.

'Sheikh, those buggers are here with wreaths. To see our Raul. We haven't let them in. Satheeshan has blocked them at the gates. The police have also arrived, hearing the ruckus. What should we do?'

'Who all are there?'

'Pandam Mustafa and that Balakrishnan Nambiar.'

'And Unni and Getto?'

'No, those backstabbers will think twice before coming here. They know that they will be slaughtered like pigs if they dare.'

'Let Mustafa and Nambiar come and see him, Arumukhan. They are not the ones who killed him, right? He died of disease. That is his fate. Also, don't say anything about Getto based on rumours. After all, he too is our boy.'

'But Sheikh, that Nambiar...' said Satheeshan, entering the room.

'Satheeshan, do you know this Balakrishnan Nambiar well? He is a poor soul, really. He landed in Kochi from Kannur right after his wedding and entered some small job at the port trust. He was a smart chap though, poor bugger. He knew that the port was where the money lay. He eventually became the chairman of the trust. This Nambiar had a brother-in-law, a first-class crook. He incited Nambiar and started a chit fund somewhere in Thrissur. He introduced all those goons from Kochi and Thrissur to Nambiar. One day, the brother-in-law played his investors and Nambiar, and went into hiding. He was in such a pickle. Somehow, he managed to avoid being charged for fraud. Rumours spread that the brother-in-law, who fled to Bombay with the money, was killed there and Nambiar was behind that murder. Slowly, Nambiar became a major player. That was how he got acquainted with this Mustafa and others. Now, Nambiar is the one who decides what trades work out in Kochi, what the obstacles are in getting them done and what one should do to overcome them, whom you should see and whom you should bribe. He is just a business consultant who charges a little bit extra. A liaison guy who gets shit done one way or the other. If you trust Nambiar and show him the money, he will get your job done. He really is a nice person. A trustworthy associate of politicians and businessmen. A clever man who knows how to divide the share in a group. He is nobody's enemy and nobody's friend. Let's not get on his wrong side. Just let them in.'

Musafir dropped the cigarette butt on the floor, crushed it under his foot and went and sat near Raul.

Pandam Mustafa and Balakrishnan Nambiar entered alongside Arumukhan. They placed the wreath on the dead body. Nambiar looked at Musafir and smiled. Musafir crossed his legs, lifted his jeans, touched the scar on his foot, smiled and looked at Mustafa. He tried to remember the scared teenager who ran away after injuring him.

'How are you, Mustafa?'

'Going well, by god's grace, Bhai.'

'Good... You should remember that this will not end with a single wreath. A foreigner has landed in Kochi, sent by the company. She is here to gauge our colour, weight and height and make a list. The game has just begun, Mustafa. By god, this is not going to end in one grave alone.'

Nambiar's face was as pale as paper. Noticing this, Mustafa held his hand. Musafir instructed Satheeshan to not let anyone inside and to call him when it was time. They went into the inner room. Satheeshan closed the door and went to sit on the chair near Raul. He looked at Raul's face and tried to imagine himself as a gangster hero in a Hollywood film. He saw his life as an action thriller projected on the white sheet wrapping Raul's body. He heard Satheeshan's character telling him about his own life story.

'Ever since I was a child, I wanted to join a gang like this. In all my childhood games, I would grab a plastic gun or a wooden knife and become a thief or a goon. I won in all those games by either hiding or fighting the police played by my friends. Moral stories and superheroes bored me. I always identified with the villain. I hated the superhero precisely because of that. The only hero I was interested in was Batman. He is not a superhero. He doesn't produce sticky webs, nor does he fly in the sky. He doesn't have any magical powers at all. Every night I went to sleep and dreamt that I would defeat him one day and conquer the city of Gotham. When a heroine got kidnapped, when the hero's sister was raped, when his mother was hit by a car or his father was shot, I transformed into the villain on the screen. When the villain got thrashed by the police, I used to feel his pain. When I got tired of always seeing the villain lose, I shifted my attention to the hero who was a goon or a serial killer. I learned something from the movies I watched. Two important circumstances are imperative in the creation of a gangster. First, his father should be an honest and a judicious man killed by the mafia or some other evil. Second, after the father's death, the mother should be forced to become a whore to raise her son. Hated by society, he will grow up to become a gangster, walk around with a gun and kill all those who stood against him. I used to observe all those gangster heroes in the movies my father brought home. Their family stories aligned with this narrative pretty much in every case. However, my father was merely a corrupt government servant, and my mother was an obedient housewife. I was sure that nobody would kill my father, and therefore my mother would never have to leave her kitchen.'

Satheeshan shifted a bit and ran his hand over his face, as if pondering from where to pick up the narrative. His 'character' began again.

'I often dream about my growth from a gangster to a gang leader. In an oft-repeated dream, a gang kills my father. My mother becomes a whore. I leave my home and join the gang. In the beginning, I take care of very small operations. One day, during an attack against our gang, while saving the leader from danger, I am shot. Once I recover from that, I become the leader's right-hand man. I go on to take part in many major operations alongside the leader, and we cleverly escape together. The gang members are bothered and jealous at my quick elevation. Some of them conspire and murder the leader. I butcher all of them and take charge of the gang.'

Satheeshan pauses to take breath.

'One night, after an operation, I escape the police and enter a busy whorehouse in the city. In the dim light inside the building, nobody can see anybody's face clearly. The women are picked according to the size and shape of their body parts, and people disappear with them into darker rooms. I have to get into one of these rooms and hide before the police arrive. I dump a wad of cash at the man bargaining in front of the rooms, open a door and enter a small room. The woman inside the room is startled out of the bed. Even in the darkness, I can see her getting out of her clothes. I grab a jug of water kept in the corner and drink. She turns the light on, and I turn back. It is my mother. She is behaving as though she has lost her mind, as if I am any random customer of hers. She makes me sit on the bed. When I resist, she holds my hands. I have to get away from the room, from my mother, from the police searching for me outside. When she tries to unbutton my jeans and undress me, I grab my gun. I kick her away and fire at her. I look at her empty eyes and keep firing.'

Satheeshan nods to himself, as if trying to convince the listener of the ways of fate.

'All I want is to escape from that filthy situation. It is like I am in a dream...in a hyper-dramatic Hollywood movie. The last shot brings me to my senses. I wake up. I am confused... Is this real or a dream? The only way I can be sure that it was a dream is if I do not have a gun in my hand. I don't know what happens after that in the dream... I cannot even guess. Had I not fired the last bullet, I wouldn't have got out of the dream. Even if I had removed that sixth bullet, I had made fatal wounds on her, and she would have died. I keep reminding myself that the next time I dream, I will fire one less round so I can find out what happens next. Yet, every time, I fire more than I had planned and wake up right after that.'

Whoever said that truth was stranger than fiction obviously never had a dream like this.

'Things moved to the clichéd movie script pretty soon,' Satheeshan went on. 'The skirmishes between Raul and Mustafa were getting uglier, as both gangs were dealing with clearing out a slum for a factory site. My father's department had prepared in advance to evacuate the slum. Two gangs were ready to act on call, one appointed by the factory management to aid those who were clearing out the slum and another hired by some traders and politicians, ready to stop that eviction activity. Raul had received the contract from the factory management to lead one group. Both gangs needed to be seen as the ones who did their job. Both the groups progressed with the fear of an attack any time. One night, while returning home, my father was stabbed to death. Meanwhile, the government intervened and evacuated the slum. Since Raul had the responsibility of protecting my father, he felt responsible for his death. He had a soft corner towards the son of someone his opponents had murdered, which made my entry into his gang easy. It was with Lothar from Mattancherry that I went to talk to Raul about joining the gang.

'"Have you really thought this through?"

'That was the only question he had for me. I nodded my head. We took a bike and reached Musafir's place. The northeasterner Getto was present with Musafir. Raul talked about initiating me into the gang, while Musafir talked on behalf of Getto. When everything was confirmed, Musafir smiled at me and called everyone else in to introduce Getto and me. Musafir, Unni, the twin Arumukhans and the rest of the gang were present. After the introductions, Musafir asked Getto and me to stretch out our left palms, and we obeyed. He asked us to hit the outstretched palm first with the little finger, then with two fingers and so on, in a steady progression, till we reached a full-fledged clap of hands. Our first lesson, designed for every newcomer, was about the unity of the gang, taught through the sound variations of our claps. Gang members were to obey three rules. One, *no member should, knowingly or unknowingly, support any activity that is harmful to the gang.* Two, *one must protect the secrets of the gang even at the cost of one's own life.* Three, *never forget these two rules at any cost.*

'I started working with Musafir, and Getto was attached to Unni. I never went back home or enquired about my mother after joining the gang. I even felt that all my life this far had been a journey towards this. I worked hard and with great commitment. Musafir was an exceptional trainer who transformed me within a short period. I kept having the dream where I woke up at the sixth bullet. In my dreams, I practised protecting Raul from getting shot at. My duties in the gang were mere repetitions of what I practised in my dreams. My dreams helped me operate in real life with perfect precision.

'We were attacked at Thoppumpady when we were returning after fixing a deal with a Marwari moneylender. Unni was our driver that day. Raul, Getto and two others were inside the jeep. Since I had foreseen this incident many times before in my sleep, I was not disturbed. I dealt with them with moves I had already planned and practised. I was sure that Raul was going to get shot at. Falling to the ground while shielding him, I took a bullet on my shoulder. The attackers fled the scene immediately. I dragged myself into the jeep, bleeding, and they left the location without wasting any time. At the hospital, Raul, Musafir and the twin Arumukhans took turns to attend to me, while the rest of them visited often. I spent eight days in the hospital, and another one and a half months resting at Musafir's house before I could actively join the gang. I became a part of all the major secret discussions of the gang. It was around that time that Unni pleaded guilty and went to jail for the murder of Sola, the daughter of Lothar from Mattancherry. Ever since Unni was imprisoned, Getto started committing to operations and carrying them out alone and with great care. A natural competition started between us.

'Unni never joined the gang full-time after returning from jail five years later. One cannot say that he left the gang, as he often worked as a middleman between the gang and others. His major business was an escort service he ran in the guise of a friendship network. The city called him "Pennunni", Unni with the women. When it got too hot for him with police raids, he started looking for other profitable businesses and attached himself to real estate. The city of Kochi was completely under the control of the real estate mafia and fourth-generation banks. From Pennunni, he became "Mannunni", Unni with the land, buying wastelands and reselling flats.

'Along with the changing city, Raul and his gang also started facing bad times. One of the twin Arumukhans, who betted and played for the gang, got murdered. Musafir was constantly locked up in the mental hospital. Raul became a weak player since he was constantly troubled by his illnesses. The gang members started getting caught by the police and attacked by Mustafa's people.'

Arumukhan's voice broke Satheeshan's train of thoughts, and he woke up with a start. Grusha had returned to Musafir's house. When the priest finished his prayers, Rita stopped chanting from her prayerbook, reminding everyone that it was time for the funeral. Satheeshan went in to call Musafir. He was finishing his last joint and a poem. He placed the poem in Satheeshan's hands.

Someone coughed loudly,
Yet who thought that it was the gunshot
To start the race?
Who started running,
Staring at his own feet,
For he was scared of the long white track lines?
Who was the last runner
Who tripped on the ribbon
The winner left?
When you light a cigarette,
Think about it for the first time
And take a long drag through your tears,
Another cough will get stuck in your throat.
You enter the bathroom and shut the door
To muffle that one.
Your fingers, shivering, unable to even tap the ash
Out of your cigarette,

Whimpering all the way.
While the ash falls on the floor,
You realize that the smoke that you inhaled refuses to emerge,
And you see the sad scene in the mirror,
Behind the soap-encrusted layers,
The images of dead people
Smoking.
When a boy comes knocking on the door,
That one with the third piece of a halved apple,
How will you escape and never let him see
Those crying pig-faced ghosts?
How can you turn yourself into a cigarette butt
And escape from him?

Satheeshan felt that it was a bad poem. He couldn't say that it was as good as Musafir's other poems. Musafir didn't care whether you told him his poems were good or bad. For him, all those poems were a way of escaping from an impending bout of madness. His discarded half-baked notes and poems were as emotionless as those medicines for depression he threw away without completing their course when he escaped his madness.

Musafir came out of the room sleepily. Arumukhan and Satheeshan eased Raul into the coffin. The funeral procession progressed to the church though a drizzle, while television channels celebrated Raul's death. A medicine-scented woman watched the news, stabbing at the keys of the remote to sift through various channels while tears blinded her eyes.

6

Move Aside

The next day, Arumukhan accompanied Grusha on her way to meet Bappu. The shock of Raul's death was still etched on his countenance. Grusha was amused at the prospect of Musafir sending the scared young man as her protector. Arumukhan assumed her smile to be a friendly gesture towards him and smiled back. Not even a smile could bridge the distance between them engineered by language and cultures. Grusha turned her attention from Arumukhan's bruised left hand, opened her laptop and turned to the file that talked about his life.

Before the battered Pandrand Albert started selling flowers, Simon had rented the flower shop in Semitherimukku to Saraswatiyamma. Her husband had abandoned her because she couldn't bear a child. Simon had helped her build her life on her own. Murukesan from Coimbatore was an agent who supplied jasmine flowers to Palakkad, Thrissur and Kochi. In the fourth month after he started his flower business with Saraswatiyamma, Murukesan became her lover. The news about his pregnant wife Chinnathai in Coimbatore never bothered Saraswatiyamma at all. He would come to her at least once a week in his lorry loaded with flowers. He would talk to Saraswatiyamma in Tamil-accented Malayalam with so much love. He carried about him the smell of jasmine flowers, engine oil and arrack. He spent the entire day hugging Saraswatiyamma in her flower shop. Their bodies smelled of marigolds; the bite of amaranth flowers assailed their noses.

In his Coimbatore home, hearing his wife's cries of pain during labour, Murukesan could not bear it and called out to his family god: 'Arumukha, take care of their lives.' Chinnathai gave birth to a boy. The baby, with his shiny dark body and glistening black hair, screamed aloud. The midwife bathed the child and brought him to the father. Relieved to see the child, the father named him after the god he had beseeched. Arumukhan. When the fortune-teller announced that the birth of the child might lead to his father's death, its grandmother Maari cursed and started to beat her own chest. She abused Chinnathai. Unable to take the constant abuse, Chinnathai jumped into a well and killed herself.

Arumukhan cried next to his mother's body that was swollen from its time inside the well. As part of the custom, along with Arumukhan, Murukesan too shaved his head. After cremating Chinnathai's body, Murukesan walked towards an arrack shop, all the while crying like a baby. Arumukhan lay attached to him like an extra body part. Murukesan sat on a rock near the place where the arrack was being distilled, laid Arumukhan down on his lap and started drinking. The hungry and tired baby licked Murukesan's chest to wet his lips. When the little baby tongue touched his nipples, Murukesan felt tickled. He laughed. The arrack ran out of his mouth and dribbled over his chest. When he tasted the arrack mixed with sweat, Arumukhan flinched in distaste and cried. Murukesan reached home, swaying unsteadily. Maari started to curse when she saw her son's plight and demanded that the baby be sent to his mother's house.

'Why do we need that kid? He is going to cause your death.'

'Chinnathai died because of your poisonous tongue. Still, you won't give it a rest, you wicked witch!'

Murukesan grabbed the old woman's hair and slammed her face against the wall. Maari started bleeding through her nose. Seeing this, Murukesan's brother beat him up and threw him out of the house. Murukesan picked up the baby Arumukhan and left Coimbatore, never to return to his old home. Saraswatiyamma was startled to see Murukesan, who had left for his wife's childbirth, return with a tonsured head and a baby. She asked him many questions, but he summed it up all in a single line: 'Chinnathai is no more.'

Saraswatiyamma took Arumukhan in her arms and kissed him on the forehead. The father and son cried on her bosom for a long time until they were tired. She caressed her lover's head with her flower-scented fingers. Murukesan felt all his sorrows being washed away. He hugged her, and they smelled of flowers together. They sold flowers together.

They had the weaning ceremony for Arumukhan in his sixth month at Guruvayoor temple. On their way back, they went into a movie theatre at Thrissur to watch a new Tamil release, *Ponnu Oorukku Puthussu*. In the middle of the movie, Saraswatiyamma went out twice to vomit. 'It's because of the long bus ride,'

Murukesan said, trying to soothe her discomfort. She whispered in his ears that there might be another reason for it. The song '*Oram po, oram po, Rukkumani vandi varudhu*' [Move aside, move aside, a vehicle named Rukmini is coming] was playing onscreen. Saraswatiyamma smiled scornfully, thinking about the old husband who left her because she couldn't conceive. Murukesan was happy at the prospect of another child. He stood Arumukhan on his lap and started making him dance to the tune.

> *Paalayam Pannaipuram Chinnathaayi peththa magan*
> *Pichai muthu eriyae varaandoi...*
> [Chinnathai's son Pichamuth, who hails from Pannaipuram,
> is coming in that vehicle...]

Unaware of the impending arrival of his sibling, Chinnathai's son Arumukhan danced on his yet unsteady legs to the beat of the song created by the famous sons of the other Chinnathai from Pannaipuram, Ilaiyaraaja and Gangai Amaran. Later, whenever the song played, Arumukhan would move his body to its tune. Arumukhan's brother was born on the day All India Radio banned that song. Later he listened to that song occasionally through Radio Ceylon.

Murukesan named his second son Arumukhan as well. Saraswatiyamma teased him, saying he was crazy to do so.

'Yes, I am crazy. But let me tell you something. I have two children. My love for them is also equal. It should be the same for you as well. Both of them are our sons. Double Arumukhan.'

Saraswatiyamma listened to her husband and raised both their sons accordingly. The younger Arumukhan looked exactly like the elder one. People talked about how both the kids were exact replicas of their father, with no resemblance to their two separate mothers. Murukesan and Saraswatiyamma named them with two separate spellings, one with an extra 'a', just to know who was who.

The Arumukhans... The elder one was a simpleton, but the younger one was quite the troublemaker. Yet they loved each other. When they were admitted to a school together, even their teachers assumed them to be twins. To avoid the technical difficulties of having two children with the same name and same initials, the headmaster added an extra letter to the spelling of one child, making one Arumukhan and the other Aarumukhan. That was the only difference they had. They were the same in body and spirit. Twin Arumukhans. Even though they were not good at their studies, no one could beat them in play. The younger one was always spoiling for a fight if any of those dejected losers decided to pick one. Once the fight intensified, the elder one would intervene. When teachers summoned them for getting into a fight, the elder one would always take the blame.

They would bunk classes and go to watch movies together. In the dark, they would sit together, munch peanuts and watch Hindi and Tamil movies in which twin brothers got separated in childhood, reunited later and fought a villain together. Even though the astrologer had prophesied that the elder Arumukhan's father would die soon after he was born, Murukesan eventually died when the elder Arumukhan was fifteen.

He had been undergoing treatment for more than a year for an infected leg, a side-effect of his diabetes. Saraswatiyamma stopped her flower business, gave up the shop she had rented from Simon and sat next to Murukesan all the time he was ill. His leg was amputated at the knee. As he lay on his bed in the hospital, the Arumukhan twins knelt on either side of him and cried. Murukesan caressed their heads and looked at the elder one.

'Dey, you should be taking care of your mother and your brother. I am going away, my dear!'

That conversation was too much for Arumukhan to bear. He whimpered. The younger Arumukhan felt like he was trapped in a melodramatic Tamil film. Murukesan consoled Saraswatiyamma, who kept wiping her tears with the end of her sari.

'Why would you cry? Even if I die, you have two boys as good as a lion and a tiger.'

The elder Arumukhan stopped his studies and started helping his mother make garlands of jasmine and tulsi at home. They joined the Tamil roadside vendors outside the Paramara Devi temple at Ernakulam North and started selling their flower garlands. When they returned home in the evening, the coins that clanged in his pocket reminded Arumukhan of the duties his father had entrusted to him.

Murukesan's condition was worsening by the minute. The infection was spreading through his body. Instead of the scent of jasmine, engine oil and arrack, the air around him was filled with his body's rotten stench. He babbled nonsense whenever his memory failed. Until the day Murukesan died, Arumukhan believed that Saraswatiyamma was his own mother. On the day his father passed away, Arumukhan was by his side. In his unconscious state, Murukesan screamed Chinnathai's name.

When his memory returned, Arumukhan fed him warm rice gruel. While his father was painfully swallowing his food, Arumukhan enquired about the name he had uttered. Murukesan coughed, and a rice grain got stuck in his nasal cavity. The watery gruel sputtered through his nostrils. Arumukhan patted his father's back and offered him water. He drank that, massaged his chest and then started to tell the story of Chinnathai. Arumukhan laid his head on Murukesan's chest and cried uncontrollably. Murukesan smiled and remembered the baby who had licked his chest the day Chinnathai died. From his laboured breathing, Arumukhan was sure that his father was dying, yet he was afraid to look at his father's face. Arumukhan closed his eyes, whimpered and repeatedly kissed his father's hairy chest. He moved away from his father's lifeless body and screamed with the pain of the death of both his parents.

Murukesan was cremated at the public burning grounds. His brother and grandmother arrived from Coimbatore and were amazed to see two sons who looked exactly the same. Maari asked Saraswatiyamma about Chinnathai's son.

'Which Chinnathai? Which son? I gave birth to both my sons!'

Even though the elder Arumukhan was happy to hear Saraswatiyamma say that, he was also quite pained at the thought that it negated the existence of his birth mother, Chinnathai. For the first time, he cursed his father in his mind.

'Why did my father tell me this when he was about to die? If he had hidden it till now, why reveal it at all? I was happy to have just one father and one mother.'

Arumukhan moved to one corner of the grounds and sat down. Seeing him cry, the younger Arumukhan went to console him.

'Anna, please don't cry. Appa needn't suffer any more now. Think like that, and please stop crying.'

After Murukesan's demise, Saraswatiyamma stayed mostly at home. In the afternoons, she would go to Semitherimukku, where the flowers would be waiting for her in the flower shop now run by Pandrand Albert. She picked them up, paid and came back home to make garlands. The elder Arumukhan would sell them in front of the Paramara temple in the mornings and evenings. At noon, he would go to the Ernakulam market and help the merchants unload their wares. During breaks from the work, while people made small talk involving politics or sleazy jokes about women, he went by himself and sat on a cement platform near the large drain that ran through the middle of the marketplace. He observed how anything thrown into the drain turned black over time and merged with the sewage. He sat next to the drain, while the rest of the world closed their nostrils at the stench rising from it. He would forget the sweet smell of the garlands he sold. It struck him that their lives were of the same ash-black shade of the sewage. He remembered his dead mother while staring at that stagnant pool of grey water. He trained himself to contain all his doubts and troubles within himself while looking at the vermin in the sewage and the moss that grew by its side.

From the profit he made from the festival sales at Paramara temple, he brought himself a tape recorder. Chinthamani, a girl who sold flowers, gave him the audiocassette of *Dalapathi*. She would look at him and smile shyly. He would then imagine that footpath of flowers, with its commotion of crowds, suddenly transforming into the blackened sewage canal. They would both metamorphose into drain worms, bubbling with love and smelling of jasmine flowers.

Both the Arumukhans squabbled over the songs from the cassette Chinthamani gave. The young one constantly listened to 'Kattu kuyilu manasukkulle' (Inside the mind of a cuckoo who lives in the forest), while the elder one was mesmerized by 'Chinna thayaval thantha rasave' (Dear one from a young mother and a king). Whenever he listened to it, the elder one would remember what his father had told him with his last breath. But before the sad song ended, the younger one would fast-forward to 'Kattu kuyilu'. While they were arguing about this, the song 'Chinna thayaval' would finish and 'Rakkamma kaiya thattu' (Clap your hands) would have begun. By that time, the elder would have calmed down and would remember Chinthamani. She used to hum this song all the time. Once that song finished, the younger one would go back to 'Kattu kuyilu' yet again. The elder one would mutter about how he wished the cassette had only two songs in it. Once while 'Chinna thayaval' was playing, the tape got stuck inside the cassette as the young one fast-forwarded it. Arumukhan slapped his younger brother, who was holding the tape in his hand. The young one, angry at his elder brother, refused to eat his dinner and went to sleep. Yet, the next day, he found the tape hanging on his cycle's handlebars like a pompom which made a pleasant noise every time he speeded up. He forgot his fight with his brother.

After his elder brother left school, the younger one started to fail in most of the games. All those they had defeated started to make fun of him. He started picking fights with them. School began to bore him. He told his mother and his brother about his plans to stop his studies.

'Didn't you listen to what Appa told me before he died? I am enough to take care of both you and our mother. After all, it is just a matter of one more year to reach class tenth.'

Arumukhan obeyed his elder brother. However, he was thrown out of the school for getting into constant fights with other students. That was how the younger Arumukhan became an apprentice at Pandrand Albert's flower shop. After he got an assistant, Albert spent very little time in his shop. All the while, he coughed incessantly and cursed Bappu, who had ruined his health. Arumukhan slowly took over the full responsibility of that shop and handed over the exact share of the profit to Albert. Arumukhan started to earn more than his elder brother.

Both the Arumukhans would stay away from their businesses on the days when new movies were released. They would stand in the long queue to buy a bunch of tickets and sell the matinee and first-show tickets in the black market for double or triple the amount, get drunk with all the money, watch the second show and return home. By the time they got back, Saraswatiyamma would be waiting for them angrily with their dinner. She would mutter things like, 'The boys are getting out of hand because their father is no more! Eat your dinner if you want.' Then she would go back to her bed, remember Murukesan and cry.

Arumukhan tattooed Chinthamani's name on his wrist the day he kissed her for the first time in the darkness of a movie theatre. Rather than tattooed, it would be correct to say that he burned her name into his skin. He lettered her name in English with little sticks on his wrist and lit them on fire. When the pain of burning skin became unbearable, he shook the burnt sticks off. By that time, the name CHINTHAMANI was embossed on his wrist. On the third day, pus oozed out of the burn. It healed in a week's time. On his dark arm, her name lay visible. He showed it to her in front of the temple that day and told her, 'Had I been fairer, your name would have been shinier than this.'

When an illegally stored bomb accidentally blasted in their shop, Pandrand Albert and his brother Simon died, leaving Arumukhan and his co-worker, Getto, jobless. The younger Arumukhan started spending most of his time with the gamblers. Whenever he played alone, he lost. But he won handsomely whenever he could manage to get his brother to play with him. The elder Arumukhan also left his job at the market and became a gambler. He continued to sell his flowers in front of the temple every morning and evening, just to meet Chinthamani. The twin Arumukhans made a lot of money from the game. If anyone raised their voice or cheated, the younger one would pick a fight. Their names got registered in the list of notorious gamblers at the police station. Whenever they were caught by the police in their raids, Sheikh Musafir used to bail them out.

The elder of the Arumukhans had met Musafir by sheer coincidence. Even though he had often seen Musafir in the city, complete with his tough looks, slanted gait and his constantly fuming cigarette, he had always moved away in fear. He had heard about this mad gangster in Raul's gang from the other labourers at the marketplace. One morning, while selling flowers in front of the temple, Arumukhan noticed a crowd running towards Veekshanam Road. He asked Chinthamani to take care of his flowers and rushed to join the crowd. He saw the gang leader Shashidharan's corpse. Musafir was wailing by the side of the dead body. Arumukhan had seen them talking to each other near the town hall the day before.

Someone had lifted up Musafir, who had fainted, and called Arumukhan to help. That stranger and Arumukhan together got an autorickshaw and took Musafir to his home at Kadavanthra. On the way, Musafir gained consciousness and looked at Arumukhan, struggling to understand who he was. He then started talking to the other person with them. It was only then that Arumukhan realized that the other person too was a gangster.

After a couple of months, Arumukhan met Musafir at a police station. Musafir was there to bail out a fellow gang member, and he recognized one of the two Arumukhans who were locked up at that time.

'Wasn't it you who took me home?' He walked to the lock-up. Arumukhan nodded his head, trying to smile. The writer at the station told him that the Arumukhans had been arrested for selling tickets for a new movie in black outside Kavitha Theatre. Musafir asked the head constable to bail out Arumukhan as well. Once he was out of the lock-up, Arumukhan requested Musafir to bail his brother out as well.

'Bhai, are you bailing out all the motherfuckers in the lock-up today? It is disgraceful for a police station to have an empty lock-up.'

Musafir half-smiled at the joke.

One evening, Arumukhan couldn't find Chinthamani outside the Paramara temple. Chinthamani used to come to work even when she was unwell. This bothered Arumukhan. When he saw her the next morning, she sadly informed him that her family had fixed her marriage with her mother's brother, as was customary. Tears welled up in her eyes, and the seventeen-year-old boy stared at the letters on his wrist. He wondered whether he should talk to his family about her. He hadn't revealed his love affair even to his brother. When he realized that he did not have the strength to struggle with anyone to make her his own, he buried his desires within. Chinthamani was married to her uncle Selvan, who sold undergarments on the footpath at Menaka Junction. Arumukhan had seen Selvan many times before on the road, calling lady passers-by to check out the undergarments, stretching the elastic with a lewd smile.

After their marriage, Chinthamani stopped selling flowers. Arumukhan completely stopped hanging out near the temple. Both the Arumukhans became full-time gamblers. They got into fights constantly. Whenever they won big, they were attacked on their way back. The elder one turned to Musafir for protection, and Musafir informed the gang about them. That was how the twin Arumukhans became gamblers for the gang. They stopped betting for fives and tens, and started playing at the prime gambling spots in the city, becoming major resource builders for the gang. They shared half of whatever they earned with the gang in return for protection. Apart from this, they were never part of any of the gang's operations. Their hands only handled cards and never touched any weapons. They were magicians calling upon djinns while throwing in their jacks and jokers.

The twin Arumukhans built a new home near Ponnurunni. The younger Arumukhan had started investing in the chit fund with Unni by that time. The elder one did not care about meddling with money transactions and interest rates, and stayed out of all that.

'Don't trust that asshole. Unni is not a fair player at all. Even Musafir Bhai does not like his pimping and money laundering. Unni is surviving only because he once had a good relationship with Raul.'

Arumukhan knew that what his elder brother said made sense. Yet he was unwilling to give up his relationship with Unni. He could only think about the women Unni arranged for him without his brother's knowledge. Unni was fascinated by women. He used to pimp women to policemen, politicians and other rich men on behalf of the gang. When he came to know about new dealers and middlemen starting the same racket in town, Unni, the younger Arumukhan and other gang members would go to their lodgings immediately. Disguised as policemen, they would fake a raid and beat up the new guys. They would get hold of the money and the jewellery from them amidst the commotion. Thinking of the shame if word got out, the new dealers would give up everything. The women would eventually come under Unni's control.

Even though Musafir had his differences with Unni, given his role in the city's underbelly, even he couldn't avoid dealing with Unni. Unni used to station his customers in an old lodge near the North overbridge. In the evening, he would often go out with them. Unni's women would have reached the Paramara temple by then. It was the time customers selected their women for the night. Unni would fix the rates for each of them with his customers. The women would accompany Unni's customers to another house he owned in Kaloor and spend the night there. Even though the younger Arumukhan often accompanied Unni during these trips, he would most often walk about the temple and not take part in any of Unni's dealings. It was his daily practice to buy a jasmine garland from a Tamil girl who had just started selling flowers outside the temple. When he became a regular, she once asked Arumukhan, 'Whom do you buy these flowers for?'

'It is for his wife, girl. If he doesn't bring her flowers, she will be cross and turn away from him in bed. No action... Do you understand?' Unni replied, ogling at the thirteen-year-old's body.

'Really? It's for your wife?' she said.

Arumukhan smiled and nodded.

'What's your name?'

'Poonkodi.'

'Good...flower vine...it's a perfect name for a flower girl.' When Unni teased her again, she reacted with a frown. Ignoring him, she turned to Arumukhan and said in a low voice, 'Here, there are more flowers in this one. Give my regards to your wife.'

Before Raul emerged as the head of the gang, most of the gambling centres in the city were under the control of Pandam Mustafa. Both the Arumukhans avoided those places. Once, they were charged with attempted murder at a gambling centre in Willingdon Island and were imprisoned. The gang came to their rescue and got them out on bail. Saraswatiyamma started pressuring her sons to get married. She wanted to arrange for both their weddings to happen on the same day.

The elder one would have nothing to do with it. 'See if he wants to get married. I don't want to get married right now. I can't even live on my own, how can I bear the burden of a girl along with that?'

The younger one's marriage was fixed with a girl from Kathirikkadavu. On the festival day at Paramara temple, Arumukhan was getting out of the temple with his fiancée when Poonkodi came running to him.

'He buys flowers for you every day from me, dear sister. I know that you like jasmine flowers a lot. Isn't it a festival here today? Today's flowers are free for you.'

Arumukhan's fiancée was perplexed. She picked a fight with Arumukhan about the mystery woman for whom he bought flowers every day. The girl left with her friends after curtly telling him that she needed to think again before getting herself attached to a man who spent time with random women.

'Why is she angry with you?'

Arumukhan did not reply but angrily left on his bike. He made for Unni's house. Unni was drinking alone. Arumukhan gulped down two shots as soon as he saw Unni's bottle and then sat down to describe all that had happened at the temple.

'You deserve this! You were the one who was overly sympathetic to her for being Tamil just because your father was from Coimbatore. What was all the drama till now? Buying flowers every day and cracking jokes and whatnot?'

'I didn't ever imagine that the little cunt would talk like this. The other one said she needs to think about this now. It's all ruined.'

'Don't worry. We will discuss with her family and work it out. Now you drink this.'

Arumukhan took the glass from Unni and gulped it down in one go. Unni asked him, 'How about we pick the little cunt up tonight? We really need to punish her. I am tired of fucking these fair and fat bitches. This girl is good, dark and really young. You just need to work on her a little hard. Are you ready?'

'What are you saying?'

'We will pick her up and will go on a long drive to Munnar. How about that?'

Arumukhan was really high by that time. He agreed half-heartedly, and they went north in Unni's Ambassador. He stopped his car in front of the town hall and told Arumukhan, 'You call her here. She won't be suspicious if you call her. If she sees me, she'll smell something wrong.'

Arumukhan opened the door and got down. Unni honked. When the girl heard the sound and looked back, Arumukhan gestured to her to come closer. *Why?* she gestured back. He pointed towards the picture of the god in front of the car and gestured that they needed flowers for the picture. The girl crossed the road with flowers. When she approached the car, Arumukhan covered her mouth and pushed her inside. Unni pressed on the accelerator.

It started pouring. Because of the faulty wiper, the scrambled lights in the rain and being high on alcohol, Unni found it difficult to drive. Whenever Poonkodi got out of Arumukhan's clutches, she pulled Unni's head backwards and the car skidded away from control. The song 'Telephone Mani pol sirippaval ivala' (Doesn't she laugh like a telephone bell?), blaring from the car stereo out of an A.R. Rahman hits cassette, drowned her screams. By the time the car crossed Kothamangalam, Poonkodi gave up fighting. Arumukhan let her go and stretched his arms. Drawing upon the final reserves of strength left in her, Poonkodi opened the door of the car and jumped out, rolling over the road like a wet bundle of clothes. Looking back out of the window, Unni tried to stop the car, which crashed onto a divider. Unni and Arumukhan jumped out of the car.

Arumukhan tried to lift her up. She had fainted. The blood flowing from her head mixed with the rain.

'We cannot take this thing to Munnar in this state. Let's finish our business fast enough, dump her somewhere here and go back. You take her to the car. I will wait outside. If some vehicles notice us, it will become a big deal. You go first. You fellow Tamilians get together. I will stay out of it for now.'

Unni took a cigarette from his pocket, shielded it from the rain with his palm, lit it and smiled at Arumukhan. Unni's face in the ghostly light frightened Arumukhan. He lifted Poonkodi up and took her to the car.

Unni's cigarette went out multiple times in the rain, and he kept on relighting it. Whenever a vehicle passed them, he squatted down and pretended to pee. Arumukhan came out of the car. It was Unni's turn next. He patted Arumukhan's shoulder with an ugly smirk, handed over the cigarette and the lighter, and closed the door. Arumukhan sat down on a milestone which recorded the distance to Munnar. While he was lighting the cigarette, he noticed the bloodstains on his shirt. He threw away the cigarette and tried to wash out the stain in the rain.

Unni opened the door and ran towards Arumukhan.

'Hey, she is gone.'

'What?'

'Dead for sure.'

Arumukhan ran towards the car. Poonkodi had bled to death in the back seat of the car.

'What do we do with her now?' Arumukhan's voice broke as he asked that question.

'What do we do? We can't get her funeral rites done, can we? We will hide her in the forest and go back.'

They picked her body up and tossed her into the dense shrubs. They ran back to the car. Unni sat in the driver's seat and asked Arumukhan to pass him the water bottle. Arumukhan searched under the seat, found the bottle and drank most of the water in one big gulp, panting like a rabid dog. Unni snatched the bottle from him and drank the remaining water before starting the car. He drove fast down the hill. Arumukhan lay back and closed his eyes in utter shock while 'Uyire uyire' started playing from the cassette of Rahman's hits.

The elder Arumukhan was returning, dejected, from a gambling den at Panampilly Nagar after losing the game. He drank himself to oblivion to forget his loss, and a friend gave him a ride home on his motorbike. Arumukhan abused his brother, who had promised to join him for the game, and ditched him. He asked the friend to stop by the main road.

'You go back. I will walk from here. The road is not good from here. There is moonlight too.'

As he was walking homewards, he saw Unni's car stop behind him and drop off the younger one. He waited for his brother. Even though he was quite dazed from all the alcohol he had drunk, he realized from his brother's frightened look that something was wrong.

'What is it, da? Why do you look like you have seen a ghost? Haven't I told you enough not to roam around with that asshole?'

He noticed the bloodstains on his brother's shirt. He pushed his brother to the fence, caught hold of his shirt and asked him, 'Which bastard did this to you? Tell me!'

The younger one looked down and started to weep. The elder one held him close.

'Don't cry, you pig. Raul and Sheikh will pick them up tomorrow, whoever they might be. Can you recognize him? You tell me that. How did you find Unni?'

The younger Arumukhan hugged his brother and confessed everything. When he finished his story, the elder brother kicked the younger one down to the ground.

'You son of a whore, you and I became who we are after selling flowers outside that temple just like her. How could you forget that?'

The elder Arumukhan lost his mind in rage. He slapped and punched his brother. The younger one tried to push the elder away and run away. Arumukhan pulled him down. He sat on his younger brother's chest and pulled out his pocket knife.

'You don't deserve to live any more, you scoundrel.'

He came to his senses after he had stabbed his brother five or six times. When the younger one stopped moving, he sat next to the body and started to whimper. Later, he cleaned his knife on the edge of his lungi and hid it. When he remembered that their mother was waiting for them at home with food, he did not feel like going there. He walked back to the main road, hailed an auto and started out for Musafir's.

Musafir was at his home, glancing out of a window at the moonlit sky and enjoying a joint. Raul was on his bed, tossing and turning from a bad headache, trying hard to sleep. When he heard a knock late at night, Musafir hid his bronze-handled knife behind him and opened the door.

'Oh, is that you? Isn't it time for you to go home after your game?'

Arumukhan entered the house, closed the door behind him, sat down on a chair, covered his face and started to cry.

'Why are you here at this hour? What happened?'

Arumukhan confessed it all to Musafir.

'Did anyone see you?'

'No.'

'How did you get here?'

'In an auto.'

'Do you know the driver?'

'No.'

The noise brought Raul out of his attempts to sleep. He massaged his forehead, looked at both Musafir and Arumukhan and frowned. When he heard everything from Musafir, he went into his room and came out with his machete. It had a decorated handle and a scabbard of polished redwood boiled in peacock oil. Raul twisted the handle and pulled out the machete from its scabbard. He approached Arumukhan with that double-edged piece of metal. He put the sword's blade close to Arumukhan's neck and asked Musafir, 'Even if it is his own brother, he touched one among us. How can we let him go, Bhai?'

Before Musafir could stop him, Raul had swung back and lunged at Arumukhan, who stopped him with his left hand. Blood squirted out of Arumukhan's wrist. Raul tried to swing his machete again, but Musafir got hold of him. He took the weapon from him and pushed Raul away.

'He did something without thinking. That does not mean you should too. He didn't mean to kill him. He was drunk, and he made a mistake. Isn't that why he came running to us first? And what his brother did, was that right? I told you to let go of that Unni many times. Isn't this our poor Arumukhan? He came in the middle of the night, asking for our help, and we should kill him in return, eh?'

Raul went back inside the room. Musafir took a towel from the clothesline and wound it tightly around Arumukhan's wrist, held him up and helped him walk out of the house. He made Arumukhan sit in the back seat of the jeep and started the vehicle.

'While you were returning from your game, someone attacked you and your brother. He died. Someone took you to the hospital. That's what happened. This should stay between the three of us. Not even your mother... Do you understand?'

Arumukhan tried to nod his head in agreement but fainted.

When he regained consciousness, there were thirteen stitches on his left wrist. Chinthamani's name on his arm was shattered beyond recognition. Musafir stood by him in the hospital. When he opened his eyes, Musafir spoke to him gently.

'His post-mortem is going on right now. Raul will take care of everything. You should not worry. We are trying to get you discharged from the hospital before the funeral.'

'What about mother...?'

'She has been informed. She is at home.'

'Bhai, how will I face her now? How will I live without him? I have never felt that I am alone. It was in a hospital bed like this that my father made me promise that I will take good care of him. And I...'

The younger Arumukhan was cremated at the same cremation ground as his father. Raul lifted the elder one, who was crying, and took him to the jeep. They left for Musafir's place. After the death of his brother, Arumukhan was at Musafir's place most of the time. He would visit his mother once or twice in a month and give her some money. He couldn't look at her face and would leave without eating anything. Saraswatiyamma believed that he couldn't stand that house with the memories of his younger brother.

After the death of the younger one, Arumukhan started to win all the games he played. He felt that the younger one was with him in all the games, sitting next to him and revealing the opponent's hand. When he ran short of money, he participated in the smaller games of tens and fifties, and avoided the big games completely. He remembered an older self who used to sit near the crowded roadsides, selling flowers. He felt that those who sat in the vehicles that sped past him looked at him and said, '*Oram po, oram po...*' (Move aside, move aside). A frightened Arumukhan veered away from the roadside, and moved closer and closer to the wall.

7

The Boar Hunt

Grusha closed Arumukhan's file and shut her laptop. She glanced at Arumukhan with great kindness. He was immersed in the sights of the city while drumming his fingers to the beat of the music he was listening to through his headphones. Discomfited with the realization that Grusha was looking at him, he raised his eyebrows shyly in a questioning way. She closed her eyes and shrugged.

Their car reached the apartment block in Panampilly Nagar. The security guard ran to the gate. Arumukhan stepped out and informed him that they were here to meet the retired ASI Bappu. The security guard went to his room and called Bappu's apartment. Receiving a positive response, he directed them towards a space to park their car. Arumukhan gestured to Grusha that he would stay close to the car somewhere. Following the security guard's directions, she reached flat no. 7A and rang the doorbell.

A woman as old as Grusha opened the door and invited her in. In the living room, Bappu was watching a cricket match with his grandson. When Grusha entered the room with his daughter, he shook hands with her and asked her to sit. His daughter went inside to fetch sherbet. She handed the drink to Grusha and introduced herself as Bappu's youngest daughter, Laila, who was practising law in the high court. Even though it was a busy day for her at the court, she had stayed back as an interpreter for her father. Bappu reduced the volume of the TV and handed over the remote to his grandson. He turned to Grusha, the expression on his face changing suddenly. Grusha was reminded of Musafir's stories and the cries of Pandrand Albert, Raul and many others.

'Balakrishnan Nambiar had mentioned that you might come. I assume that you know me?'

'Yes, Musafir told me about you.'

'Oh! The crazy Musafir!'

'He is not crazy now.'

'I know he is not crazy. His madness is just a smokescreen to fool the court. I can imagine how he would have introduced me.' Bappu laughed, his entire body shaking with the effort.

'It is time for my prayers. You talk to Laila and begin the conversation. I will be back soon.'

Bappu went inside with his grandson for his Zuhur namaz. Laila approached Grusha with some files.

'Uppa hasn't told me anything about your visit. He is mostly silent these days. I think his psoriasis pain has also increased. Since his retirement, he has also been undergoing treatment for depression. Uppa is receiving an unusual number of phone calls these days. He is searching for copies of old case files with such enthusiasm, even late into the night. I can only assume that it must be something complicated that connects a retired policeman and the plan to start an IT company on land allotted by the government for the Info City. I do not understand any of this.'

Grusha smiled, looking into Laila's eyes, which were awaiting a response. She raised the glass of sherbet to her lips with the meditative focus of a Zen monk. Each sip Grusha took disturbed Laila. She was troubled with some unknown fear and hoped that her uppa would return soon from his namaz. Even though she was not interested in cricket, Laila fixed her eyes on the TV screen. The Indian fast bowler was abusing the Australian batsman and was prancing on the field. Bappu returned after the prayer. He looked at the TV and asked his grandson about the game.

'They stopped it, Vappachi – it's raining. This is an old one.'

Bappu nodded. He pointed at the TV and walked towards Grusha.

'Look at him... That chap is from Kochi. That's why he is behaving like that. Whether it is in cricket or in crime, this is how people from Kochi behave. They don't wait for wounds to heal.'

Bappu sat back in his chair. He had covered his shoulders with a bath towel. Laila's son snatched the towel and ran off, in an act of mischief. Grusha noticed that amidst the greying hair on his chest, all over his body and on his ears, his skin was peeling like shedding snakeskin. She also noticed how his navel was swollen. Laila ran after her son, got hold of the towel and returned it to her father. He shook it once and used it to cover his body. Whenever he fumbled in the conversation, Laila helped him out with his sentences.

'There was once a dispute between two foreign companies over a plot of land in the proposed industrial city called Info City. Both parties attempted to settle their dispute in court and outside. Since both the companies were equally powerful and had strategic contacts with political parties and the bureaucracy, the issue kept festering. That was when the various gangs of Kochi started to meddle in the affair. I only have some hints about this illegal deal...stories that are as interesting and as unbelievable as myths. They tell me that you are here to solve this dispute. Everything is hearsay. Now you tell me. How can I help?'

'You were in the police service in and around Kochi for a long time, right? You can help us for sure. I have already collected all the relevant information I need about Raul and his gang. Now I need some information about Getto, Mustafa and their gang and some background to the city of Kochi. Only then can we come to negotiating a deal that will resolve the dispute pertaining to the land once and for all. So...'

Laila interrupted.

'What's this deal you are talking about?'

Grusha put down her glass on the table like a gangster giving up his weapon. She glanced at Bappu and Laila and continued.

'Russian roulette... A final round of shots in a lethal game of chance. That is the final solution on offer. The companies are going to bet on the gangs of Kochi. The gangsters will take part in the process on behalf of these companies. This is a completely illegal settlement. But the companies and some other key players in the game have decided to settle the matter in this way.'

'Who are they?'

'I don't think you would believe me if I tell you. I don't know the exact details about it. That's the truth.'

Laila looked at Bappu in shock. He was sitting there as a good listener, with no visible expression on his face. Laila retreated to the kitchen, holding the empty glass. Bappu moved his chair closer to Grusha.

'So, what next?'

'I am responsible for conducting the roulette. As a first step, I have to compile a tentative list of all those who will take part in it and send it to the companies. Once the companies finalize that, the next step is to procure the weapons required to run the roulette. Since this kind of lethal game is prohibited, we will have to find the weapons for it illegally. I would suggest using local guns familiar to the people of Kochi. We need to find out the places or people from where we can get hold of those kinds of guns. We need to fix a location for the roulette.'

'Who all are there in your list?'

'We have planned a Russian roulette with six participants. Three of them were selected from Raul's gang earlier for one company. Sheikh Musafir. Raul. Getto. But Raul...'

'You need someone to replace Raul. You have to plan for that change. That is the way their gang also functions. Also, Getto... I am not sure if he is still a part of their gang. I heard that he had a disagreement with Raul, and I also suspect that he is the one who betrayed Raul.'

'But Musafir did not talk about any of that.'

'What does he know? He was hospitalized, right? Didn't he get out of the hospital just yesterday? Not just that, we are not clear whether what we hear about Getto is true or not. You can consider someone else from Raul's gang in place of Getto. Leave that for now. Tell me who all are there from the other gang.'

'We haven't decided that yet. I know you are well connected with Mustafa's gang. I am here to decide about that too.'

'There are no issues in that. Mustafa himself will take part in this. I would suggest Mattancherry Lothar's name next. There is no better sharp shooter in Kochi now. He is good at making local guns. The third one... Give me a day, and I will find a third one for you. You should now go and meet Lothar and Getto. Anything else?'

'I told you. I want to know the history of crime in Kochi. I need to include that in the report I am sending to the companies.'

'I have prepared a note with Laila's help. That note covers details until two years ago. You will get a basic idea about this city from that. Laila will give it to you.'

After Laila returned from the kitchen, Bappu asked her to show Grusha the note they had drafted. She handed over the file to Grusha, who started reading it:

> In Kochi, on an average, there occur about ten big crimes a day. This includes robbery, sale of weapons, drug smuggling, terrorism, trafficking of women, extortion, murder, organ trafficking, cybercrime, gambling, land mafia dealings, gang activities, political corruption, black money transactions and forgery. Never presume that this is limited to the small gangs in the city. These activities involve people outside the state and even outside the country. At least when it comes to criminals, we have complete equality here. Among the

escorts, you will find women who will undress for a hundred bucks and actresses who demand tens of thousands. You will be mistaken if you consider the vehicle robbers as a small gang. They include a big organized maze involving politicians, businessmen and policemen. In the land mafia dealings, you will find local brokers and benami (proxy) players of multinational corporations betting against each other. The fruit seller and the banker are equally susceptible to getting mugged on the streets. If you have defaulted in your loan payments, instead of the banks and police, you will be visited by gangsters.

Kochi is the crime capital of Kerala now. The city dwellers live in fear. They are scared to step out of their homes at night. They will never leave their houses locked for more than a few days. They are terrified to report a hooligan who is creating a ruckus in the movie hall. All of them have lost their trust in the police.

People have started to come together to protect themselves. They are taking the help of private agencies for their safety. The hottest job these days in Kochi is that of a private security force. You can see them everywhere in the city, sometimes unarmed and sometimes with weapons. The police force has been reduced to mere scarecrows now. There is a register for policemen who go out for night patrolling. If you take a look at it, you will realize that there are no crimes recorded in that book any more. There will be some activity right after a new commissioner has taken charge or after a major crime. But it will die down eventually. The night patrolling will get limited to the rich businessmen's localities or others who have some hold over the police department.

Grusha finished reading the note, folded it neatly and slipped it into her pocket.

'What do the gangs stand to gain from all the fear they are generating?'

'What gain? If a city is scared of barking dogs, are the dogs responsible? Or are the demons who raise the dogs in the middle of the night responsible? Or are the thieves responsible? Who is hunting the boars? The dogs or their owner Rawther?'

Grusha and Laila did not understand these questions and looked at Bappu in puzzlement. Bappu started narrating an old story.

'I had worked in the Kothamangalam police station for about three years. That is where I met Hassan Rawther. He was a watcher at a tea estate in Malakkappara. Rawther was a perfect hunter. He would often narrate his experiences of hunting. I was so mesmerized by his stories that I felt like taking part in it at least once. When Rawther's vehicle visited Kothamangalam, I would often take a lift in that on its way back and reach Malakkappara. People used to explode water bombs to catch fish. It was a common sight to meet people without hands or fingers as a result of these bombs bursting in the hands of drunk fish-seekers. Those missing a hand would still fling these bombs with their remaining hand. Those missing both their hands would light a cigarette from a teashop nearby, hold the bomb in their stumps and light it with their cigarette before throwing it into the water. Fishes would die and come up to the surface.

Their dead eyes would still be shell-shocked. Their fins would still shiver from the blast.

'He would step into his plantation on holidays, looking for game. He would only have a local gun, a machete and a crowbar sharpened at one end. I joined him out of curiosity to see how he would hunt a boar with just these minimal supplies. We drank at his home until it was pitch dark. Once it was night, we left with Rawther's youngest son. Since Rawther married late, his son was very young, about eight or ten years old. He carried the torch. Rawther walked with his gun strapped to his back and a machete in his hand. I followed him, carrying the crowbar. It was a moonlit night. Rawther whistled loudly before we turned to take the road to the plantation. I was wondering why he would do that, when a large pack of dogs joined the troop. These were not trained dogs, just plain old strays. Around fifteen of them. When we reached the middle of the plantation, we climbed a tree nearby. The dogs lay close to the tree quietly. Rawther started to load his gun. Instead of bullets, he was using the kind of iron bolts used in automobiles. He said that these would hardly pierce the fat layers of the pig. He informed us that a deep wound would make the boar dangerous and it was then an impossible feat for humans to capture it.

'We sat on the branches of the tree, waiting for the boar. Rawther started to sing in a low voice. He occasionally patted his son's head to stop him from dozing off. When we heard the movement of the pig, we became alert. Rawther's son turned the torch on that wild creature. In that short moment when the animal froze at the sudden light, Rawther's gun found its target. I thought that the animal would run back. But it snorted and ran towards the tree we were sitting in. That was when I witnessed an unbelievable sight. The dogs that had accompanied us moved towards the tree. Like a humongous sea serpent with many heads, the dogs closed in on the boar and started barking. When the boar saw a group of shiny-eyed dogs barking at it, it decided to run away. The dogs followed it.

'The boar ran frantically through the narrow plantation pathway. It was bleeding from its wound. The dogs divided themselves into three or four groups, closing in on the boar from various directions. If it managed to evade one group, it would invariably run into another. When the tired, wounded animal slowed down, the dogs attacked it from behind and bit its balls. They knew it was the only way to defeat a boar. The boar would then sit on the ground, shake its head, baring its teeth and invite the dogs for a fight. The pack of dogs would be afraid to approach the wild boar from the front and stay away. One or two of the dogs would start snapping at the boar's rear, and it would have no other option but to run again.

'The next few minutes were repeated cycles of this process. The boar was bleeding from its wounds, and eventually it sat down, tired, on the ground. Even then the dogs kept a safe distance from the boar. Rawther waited quietly until the boar could not take even one small step. He handed the gun to me and jumped from the tree with his machete and the pointed crowbar.

'The dogs crowded in front of the tired boar and barked together. Rawther crept round behind the boar, took a deep breath, mustered all his strength and thrust the crowbar through the boar's back. The pig squealed piteously and fell down. Rawther pulled out the crowbar and, with his machete, cut off the head, the tail and the feet of the animal. He slit open its belly and removed its innards. The liver belongs to the leader of the pack. That is the rule of the hunt. Rawther removed the liver and threw it to the dogs, along with the head, feet and intestines. That was the dogs' reward for participating in the hunt. They fought to get a share from what was given to them. Rawther called us, and we climbed down. We hung the boar on the crowbar and carried it back. The pack of dogs finished their meal and went back. The next day, I tasted the meat of a boar for the first time in my life. It tasted like that frightful night.'

Laila, her son and Grusha listened to that story intently. Bappu sighed, as if signalling the end of the story. He pressed the towel on his head and looked towards Grusha.

'Several boar hunts like this are happening in this city... There are many here, big ones and small ones, and then there are many stray dogs willing to bark and run behind them. And then there are these Rawthers controlling the dogs. Come to think of it, all the gangs in Kochi are mere packs of dogs. They are conquering the boar just for a piece of the liver or a tail or a long portion of the intestine. The real Rawthers, the hunters, are also here. These gangs are mere dogs waiting for the whistle.'

Bappu became silent. He was panting like a boar, tired of running. He gestured to his daughter to get him some water. When Laila got him a glass, he drank it in one gulp and closed his eyes. Grusha told him that it was time for her to leave. Bappu followed her out of the flat and entered the lift. Grusha pressed the button for the ground floor. Bappu seemed very distressed as they waited for the lift to reach down. Grusha observed him keenly.

'Balakrishnan Nambiar will call you and let you know the other details. You just listen to him. Another thing, I will be the third one to participate from Mustafa's gang. Let it be a secret for now.'

Grusha looked at him, astonished. The lift reached the ground floor, and both of them stepped out.

A cigarette glowing between his lips, Arumukhan was waiting impatiently for her next to the car. He opened the door for Grusha and stepped inside the car. The driver asked her where to go. Grusha looked at Arumukhan and told him, 'Mattancherry Lothar.' She opened her laptop and created a list of the final participants in the roulette.

Pandam Mustafa

Lothar

Bappu

Getto

Raul's replacement

She typed 'Sheikh Musafir' as the last name in the list.

After Grusha left, Bappu went to the security guard's room. Like he usually did when he was bored, he looked at the scenes from various closed-circuit TV screens, sitting at his ease as if the entire building was under his control. Wrinkles of power spread across his face. When he had stood in front of the sessions judge Fakir Mohamed at Coimbatore for the infamous Rajan case, his face had reflected the same expression.

Bappu, son of Valiyavalappil Kunjaboobakkar, joined the police force in 1974. He was born in a conservative Muslim family in Eranadu. Kunjaboobakkar was an expert in herbal treatment and Arab folk medicines to cure poisoning. Bappu was the first-born in his marriage to his second wife. Among the eight siblings, only Bappu showed an interest in learning traditional medicine from his father. Even though he wanted to study further once he passed the tenth class, his father did not allow him to continue.

So, Bappu stayed back at home and helped his father with the daily chores and continued his religious studies. He tended to the many medicinal herbs in their courtyard, such as *kunni*, *analivegam*, *erikku*, *koovalam*, *vettila* and *aryaveppu*. He quit his after-bath ritual of cleaning his ears with a tip of his towel, since earwax mixed with spittle was necessary to cure a snakebite. He stayed awake with the snakebite cases and took care not to let them drift off to sleep. He fed them peppercorns and asked them to describe the taste to measure how far the poison had spread, dripped the juice of betel leaves in their mouths and prayed for them, eventually bowing his head like a defeated soldier when some patients turned blue or red and succumbed to death.

He developed sores on his skin. His skin peeled off, and he developed ear infections. Stinking pus oozed out of his navel. Bappu's mother wept and accused his father that this was the curse of the snakes. She demanded he stop treatments involving her son. Kunjaboobakkar continued his snakebite treatment without anybody else's help.

Kunjaboobakkar became paralysed when Bappu was twenty-four years old. He passed away in a matter of three months, putting an end to the never-ending line of patients and the scent of herbs in the house.

One day, when Bappu was outside the mosque, about to go in for his Maghrib prayer, policeman Ravindran Nair came running and told him that his wife had been bitten by a snake and taken to Bappu's home. Bappu informed him that he had stopped practising and that Nair should take his wife to the hospital immediately. Ravindran Nair fell at Bappu's feet and cried. To get away from him for the time being, Bappu told him that he would come after his namaz. He spent more than the required time to cleanse himself. When the smooth floor of the mosque touched his forehead through a tear in the carpet, Bappu felt guilty. He performed *sujud* the way a medicine man would expel the poison from a patient's wound. He finished his namaz, removed the handkerchief from his head and stepped out to look for Ravindran Nair. He had assumed that Nair would have left by then. He saw Nair standing near a coconut tree with his hands crossed across his chest, his eyes closed. He heard the sounds of people coming out after their namaz, opened his eyes and rushed towards Bappu.

'Your namaz is over, right? Please come and take a look at her now.'

When they stepped into the courtyard, they could hear the cries from inside the home. The policeman hugged his daughter, who had fallen, crying, on top of her mother's corpse. When the group of people started to leave the place with the corpse, Bappu went and held the man's hand, as if asking for forgiveness.

'So what if she died; you didn't miss your namaz.'

Those words pierced Bappu's heart like a dagger. *You didn't miss your namaz*, the djinns and other mystic beings stood around him and repeated. Bappu went inside and locked the door, but the voices in his head would not go away. He ignored the peeling skin on his body and started practising medicine again. After he got married, he abandoned Arab folk medicine and concentrated only on local traditional ways of treatment. As modern medicine prospered, his earnings and the number of patients reduced considerably.

He joined the police force despite the protests from his mother and his uncles. Sixteen months after he joined, Indira Gandhi declared Emergency in India. He continued his medicine practice along with his police job. When someone took a patient to Bappu's home, someone else would run to the police station to inform him. Bappu would rush back home in his police uniform. His wife would have prepared the required medicines by that time. He would administer the necessary procedures for the patient, and then return to the station right away and continue his policing work. He would beat up criminals and political prisoners. He was a loyal servant of the government. He never asked questions – he minded his tongue and did what was asked of him. Once the Emergency was lifted, he was transferred to the Kasaba police station in Kochi.

In the beginning, Bappu was a responsible police officer in Kochi. Slowly, when he got fed up with political interference and compromises, he transformed into a true policeman who made use of the power of fear. He got closer to the politicians and the businessmen, and worked according to their desires. He beat up Albert and helped Lothar to keep his arms business going. He crafted fake reports against Musafir's gang and raided the women in Unni's group. He became an ally for the smuggling activities of Balakrishnan Nambiar and wrote feeble charge sheets whenever Pandam Mustafa got caught. He received multiple punishment transfers, memos and promotions. By the time he retired from his long twenty-one years of service, he was an assistant sub-inspector at Ernakulam South police station.

Three years after he got transferred to Kochi, he had built a home for himself in Kakkanad. It was a small town then – almost a village – where people would come looking for him to cure snakebites. Even though he got transfers all over the Ernakulam district, his wife, two daughters and son lived at Kakkanad. When he was posted at the Kasaba station, he would go home every night. Everywhere else, he would go home on the weekends. When he was at home, he would monitor the surroundings closely. If anyone loitered near the house at night, he would turn his four-battery torchlight on them, demand to know who they were, and from where, and scare them off. He made it his duty to keep the entire region under his surveillance.

Ever since Kakkanad became an industrial area, he lost his peace of mind. He couldn't question the passers-by at night any more, since workers were constantly coming and going on their various day and night shifts. After his wife's demise, he sold off his property in Kakkanad and shifted to their new home in

Panampilly Nagar. In their courtyard at Panampilly Nagar, he did not keep medicinal herbs, and neither did he have a wife to assist him. That was how Bappu stopped practising his traditional medicine the second time.

After his retirement, Bappu realized how the scent of power had rubbed off on him along with getting the star insignia on his shoulders. He became active in Mustafa's activities to consolidate some of that power. He would use his contacts and his familiarity with the police system to pass on useful information to their gang. Sitting in front of the closed-circuit television in the guard's room, his face reflected the wrinkles of an old snake. He fell into a light doze.

The security guard patted the sleeping Bappu's shoulder and pointed towards his ringing mobile phone. Bappu answered it as he walked to the lift.

'Yes, Mustafa, yes, that white girl was here too. God almighty will bring to us without fail all those we want to meet. You know that, right? Once, when I was catching hold of a bunch of gamblers, one guy managed to escape. I couldn't get him even though I ran after him for a while. We took the rest of them to the lock-up. After we reached the station, the other guy came looking for me. As it turned out, he was hiding from the police in some bushes and was bitten by a snake. I made him lie down on the table, removed the poison from him, applied the earwax paste on him and put him inside the lock-up. Whenever he fell asleep, I went inside and slapped him on his cheeks. When he realized that staying awake was important to live, every time I slapped him, he would look at me thankfully. Don't you remember how you tried all your life to hide from me and eventually came looking for me? This is an opportunity to get them all together. Call Nambiar once again. That white girl looks like she means business.'

Bappu cut the conversation short, touched his bald head and took the lift to the seventh floor.

8

Jew Street

Lothar's house was approximately half a kilometre away from Jew Street in Mattancherry. Arumukhan knew that he had a workshop somewhere nearby, where he made those local guns. Arumukhan asked the driver to stop the car a little distance from Lothar's house. He pointed towards Lothar's house and gestured as usual that he would stay with the car. Grusha got out of the car and slowly crossed the road, reached Lothar's home and rang the doorbell.

Mary had no idea why she was selected to carry the son of God. While she was listening to the angel's announcement, instead of thinking about God's great plan for her, she was bothered and worried about the shame she, a virgin, would have to suffer. She felt like crying when she thought about how God left a child to grow inside her without asking her beforehand. 'What does Joseph expect from me? What does the angel expect from me?' she kept muttering. All of Mary's anxieties were about the possible perspectives the owners of her body would take. However, Gabriel, without intervening in those anxieties she had, suggested a name for the baby and hid in the dark like a secret lover. It was only after Gabriel left that Mary wondered why God did not give her a daughter instead.

She liked girls more than boys. She had even thought about a name for a daughter, had made a little dress for her and had memorized all the songs she would sing to her daughter. She never expected this kind of a move from God. It was as if a thief had handed over his stolen property to a passer-by to avoid getting caught and fled the scene. Just like that passer-by would touch the gold, Mary lifted her dress and caressed her belly. She was scared of herself. The boy started to grow inside her, and she started to grow weaker.

Since the baby was miraculously planted within her, her own body carried on as if it were alien to her, not really her own child. So, it prepared for its own baby each month, and then discarded the preparations, as Mary was still a virgin. So she continued to menstruate. Just like the passer-by would, even amidst abject poverty, keep the gold for the thief to come back and reclaim, Mary's body functioned as pure as ever. She grew more and more suspicious of the period blood that flowed from her. She wondered if it was her period blood or the sign of an abortion. She prayed to the God, who had tricked her, to let it be an abortion. Yet when she touched the menstrual blood and inhaled its familiar scent, she cursed God. When the child moved in her belly, she would scold him and ask,

'What do you want?'

He would kick her harder from within the belly.

'You are just like your father. Why do you torture me like this? Will you tell your father that if my duties end after giving birth to you, I wish to die in childbirth?'

'Then who will feed me? Who will sing lullabies? Who will change my diapers?'

'Don't you have a father? Doesn't he have his angels? Don't they know how to perform miracles?'

'I don't want any of them. I am your son alone.'

They continued to argue for a little while longer.

Dora was adding finishing touches to her college assignment, a conversation between Mary and Immanuel, her unborn son. The doorbell rang when she was writing the final section. She stopped writing, arranged the sheets of paper and left her room. When she opened the door, she saw a young white woman. It was a common sight for Dora. A lot of tourists approached her to be their tour guide. Dora did not hesitate to start a conversation with the woman standing in front of her.

'The synagogue isn't open yet. Also, I am a little busy.'

'I am not here for you. I want to meet Lothar. Isn't this his house?'

'Yes, but Papa is not here right now. I am Ruth, his daughter. He must be in the workshop and will return only at night. Should I take a message?'

Grusha thanked her and walked back. When she reached the car, Arumukhan pointed towards another building a little ahead.

He had enquired about the workshop by then. Grusha gestured to Arumukhan to wait in the car and walked towards the workshop.

Lothar was born in Jew Street. His papa, Harry, was a bike mechanic. Lothar didn't remember his father, who had died in an accident while test driving a bike he had repaired. Lothar was a kid at the time. After his father's death, Lothar and his mother were taken in by his paternal grandfather. He raised them so they never felt the absence of his son.

Lothar's grandfather used to advise him to become a better mechanic than his father. In his free time, the boy practised on his grandfather's piano. One day, while playing the piano, his grandfather clutched his chest and fell backwards with the chair. He died instantly. Lothar and his mother lived with his uncle, his father's younger brother, after that. Thereafter, Lothar's father's elder brother Aaby took care of all the responsibilities of educating Lothar. Every month he sent some money to them. Once he passed his tenth class, Lothar informed his mother that he was going to join the polytechnic college. He wrote to Aaby that he wanted to become a good mechanic. Once his mother and Aaby agreed, he started on the tool- and die-making diploma course for three years.

At the college, the student union had been dominated by the left for eighteen years. The left organizations refused to give space to any other political party and stood as a threat to anyone who dared. Lothar's family belonged to the Congress party. Yet Lothar knew that his father had been a communist. The threatening nature of the left parties inside the college offended Lothar. Everything went peacefully until the student union elections took place in his first year.

Everything changed suddenly. Lothar's friends got beaten up since they did not take part in the campaigning for the left party. At night, the electric supply to one wing of the hostel was switched off to let people enter and beat up the inmates. There was enough faint light for the victims to identify the people who beat them. Yet the principal refused to accept their complaint since there was no proper evidence against anyone. Most of those who got beaten up started working with the left organizations, while a few became rebels. Lothar was one among the latter.

In their second year, Lothar and his friends created a panel to contest against the popular left party. Lothar was their chairman candidate. Even though Lothar lost by thirteen votes, two members from their panel won the election. Lothar became a prominent figure. One day, on his way from class, Lothar ran to the college ground when he heard there was a disturbance there. He saw a group of people beating someone black and blue. He realized that it was the college magazine editor, who had won the seat. Lothar was also beaten up when he tried to break up the fight. They left the editor and turned their attention to Lothar. His nose started to bleed. He pleaded with them to let him go, but they kicked him down to the ground. When he had no other resort, he screamed and reached behind him for the mini drafter. It was a folding metal contraption for making engineering drawings.

He swung the drafter at the head of the next guy who came after him. The measurement equipment broke off, and the metal rods remained. The one who got hit sat down on the ground and covered his head with both hands. The drafter next fell on the face of the second guy, bruising his cheeks, blood gushing out. The third guy, after getting hit on his leg, saw his friends running away. The magazine editor took the drafter from Lothar's hands and started to hit back at those who had hit him. When Lothar realized that the editor was going wild with the drafter, he grabbed it from his hands, threw it away and ran out of the campus with him.

When he went to sleep that night, he was sure that their principal, fed up of the political brouhaha on campus, would have already informed the police and they would be at his place the next morning.

He left his mother and his home that night. He only had a few rupees he had saved up and the address of his father's brother Aaby in Bombay. As he travelled in the night train to Bombay from Ernakulam South railway station, he cried, thinking about his mother whom he had abandoned and apologized in his mind to his dead grandfather.

By the time his mother received a formal-looking brown envelope with an official seal stamped on it and started reading the official letter from college with the words, 'Your son has manhandled other students of this institution...', Lothar had already reached Bombay. He wandered around and eventually found Aaby.

Lothar had believed that Aaby was a textile mill worker. As it turned out, he was a gangster on the streets of Matunga. Aaby and his wife Sara embraced Lothar and took him in like he was their own son. Tired of sitting idle at home, he joined a small Gujarati workshop on their street as an apprentice. He spent the meagre wages he earned on Bollywood films and to get drunk and go to concerts. Aaby thought of advising him to return home. Yet he realized that Lothar wouldn't go back there after his mother had married his father's younger brother. Aaby also knew that if he gave up on him, Lothar would end up on one of the streets of Bombay, which stank of blood.

When the Gujarati workshop owner passed away, Lothar took charge. The profit he made from the workshop was dutifully shared with the Gujarati's wife and their two daughters. Later, Lothar married the younger daughter. Even though Sara was against this marriage, Aaby supported them. Aaby wrote to Kochi with all the details of the marriage only after it had taken place. He did not get a response to his letter. It was Aaby who named Lothar's elder daughter Tamar and the younger one Ruth. Since Lothar was fond of his grandfather's piano, he always called his daughters Solatido and Doremifa. They grew up with the abbreviated names Sola and Dora. Every night, after work, he would get drunk and reach home in a tipsy state. Dora and Sola would run to their papa and snatch the box of sweets he had brought. He would sit back in his squeaky old chair, imagine playing an invisible piano and, when he reached the major scale, he would scream the key notes loudly:

Do... re... mi... fa...
So... la... ti... do...
Do... do... do it.

His wife would mumble from the kitchen while making rotis for their dinner. To calm her down, he would go to her, take a piece of a roti she had made, chew on it and kiss her hard on her cheek. Dora and Sola would giggle.

One of those days when he was not too busy in the workshop, Lothar took one of Aaby's discarded old guns with him to the workshop out of curiosity. He worked on it for a day and a half, and made an exact replica of the Smith and Wesson Model 36 six-shot revolver. One without any flaws. Lothar felt that he had become a great mechanic like his father.

'Did you really make this?' Aaby was still doubtful when he saw the gun. Lothar nodded to say yes. Aaby hugged him tight. His workshop became just a workshop in name. He made copies of the .36 Chief's Special and .357 Magnum, with matching bullets for them. Aaby trained him to use a revolver. Aaby's chhota gang became loaded. When they required more guns, Lothar cultivated a group around him who would make more guns. In his free time, Lothar tested his aim using the guns he made. Soon, things started to spin out of control. Aaby's group and Lothar's group started expressing their differences and even engaged in fights. They parted ways before things became worse. Yet there was mutual respect and love between Aaby and Lothar.

Lothar bought a house a little distance from Aaby's place, and shifted his workshop closer to his new place. It was a street where hijras lived. Whenever they came and demanded money, Lothar hurled abuses at them. Dora and Sola giggled when the hijras abused back and lifted their clothes in protest. Even after parting ways, whenever some big gang attacked Lothar for an arms deal gone wrong, Aaby and his gang always came to his rescue. Once a new commissioner took charge, their good times started to decline. An encounter specialist, he had decided to target the heads of the five gangs from Matunga. Lothar was the fifth one on the list. He had played his invisible piano as usual and had gone to sleep when the police circled his home and started shooting. Sola and Dora woke up from their sleep and started to cry. Lothar and his wife tried to cover their mouths. Their front door was about to give way. They realized that the only way to escape was to take the bike parked outside their back door. Lothar rounded up his wife and children and ran to the back door. He got on his bike and sat little Dora in the front on the petrol tank. His wife sat behind. Sola hid between her papa and her mama. He opened the back gate, asked for god's help, pushed the policemen aside and kick-started the bike. The policemen fired at them. His wife was shot. Sola saw her mother falling to the ground, sat quietly and hugged her father. Dora didn't know what was happening behind her. She sat in front, her little hands covering her face to block out the cold wind.

Lothar sped to the railway station and discarded the bike close by. They got into the general compartment of a train that was about to leave. Sola was hugging her father and crying, while Dora was searching for her mother in the crowd. After fourteen long years in Bombay, Lothar returned to Mattancherry with his two daughters, eight and six years old.

He was clueless for a few days and then decided to start doing the one job he was good at. He started his new workshop, and Aaby suggested the name 'Cain Lathe Works'. Aaby told him that Adam's great-grandson Tubal Cain was the first blacksmith. It was Aaby who sent the money to start the workshop. At first,

Lothar only did simple jobs, yet when he realized the needs of the city, he started making weapons again. He mainly made handy knives and swords he could conceal inside wooden rods and walking sticks. They became infamous as weapons 'made in Mattancherry'. When the city couldn't get enough of the locally made guns, he occasionally made guns as well.

Lothar walked towards Grusha, who was standing in front of the workshop. Since Pandam Mustafa had already informed him about her, Lothar was not a bit surprised to meet her. He introduced himself to Grusha.

'Bappu guided me towards you. I hope you know what this is about.'

'Yes, I know. What do you need? I hope money is not an issue for you. Are you particular about imported ones?'

'Money is not the problem. The weapon should be familiar to all the participants. It should be of the best quality. That is what we need.'

'When it comes to guns, there is only one measure of quality. If it fires, the one in front of you should die. That is all. I know how to make guns that will do the job. This is not the old times. In Kochi, the guys have all kinds of weapons with them. It's just that they don't use them that often. Since you are ready for this game, let me suggest you use the locally made ones. I will give you six beautiful copies of the .36 Chiefs.'

Grusha nodded in agreement.

'I don't keep my stock here. I will have to go and get it from where it is kept. Until then, you can wait at my place. It is close by.'

'I know. I went there first.'

Lothar walked towards his home with Grusha. When they went past Arumukhan, he turned away, towards the car, and stood still. When Lothar knocked on his door, Dora was trying to finish her assignment.

Mary hugged the pale body of her son when it was brought down from the cross, and she cried. She looked at his half-shut eyes and started to ask questions.

'Is this why your father entrusted me to carry you and raise you? He is deciding your birth and your death all by himself. Don't I have any rights over you, dear son? Why do we struggle like this for your father? Why do we suffer for him to gather praises? He gave the ark to Noah, music to David and leadership to Moses. Yet he punished you to this fate. Couldn't you escape? When Pontius Pilate asked you if you are the son of God or the king of Jews, why didn't you tell him that you are the son of Mary? Didn't I give birth to you and raise you? You have distributed your blood, your body, your words, your breath and your life for your disciples, for prostitutes, for the sick and the sinners. What is left for me in this body of yours?'

Let's go back to the bag of money and the thief. When the thief comes back to collect his money, the traveller will part with it and end up crying, not because of the money but because she was fond of the little motif on the bag. Mary was crying for a loss like that.

Dora read the portion she had written and was thinking, searching for a title, when she heard a knock on the door. She gathered the sheets of paper and left the room with them. When she reached the front door, she saw the foreigner was back, this time with her papa. Lothar introduced Grusha to his daughter.

'I am going to Kombara and will be back soon. Let her wait here till I get back.'

Dora directed Grusha towards a chair. Grusha asked her name. She introduced herself as Ruth. Only her papa called her Doremifa. Whenever he called her Ruth in public, she felt as ancient as the Holy Torah. Dora asked Grusha to settle down and went inside to make some tea. To kill time, Grusha glanced at the sheaf of papers Dora had left on the table and started reading.

'Che vuoi' – What do you want? What does God expect from us? Jews are confused about that. That is why they worry about what to do and how to react to situations. Yet they believe that they are the chosen lot. It is with this belief that they justify their actions. When a non-Jew looks at a Jew, similar questions will start swarming in his head: 'Che vuoi?' They will fabricate stories about the Jews; they will represent Shylock as the deaf man who can only listen to the clinking of the coins. They will alienate the Jews as a group that is out to conquer the world.

One can see the same anxiety between the Jews and their God. When God demanded Isaac as a sacrifice, even God was unaware, like Abraham, of the reasons for such a demand. Yet Abraham obeyed and justified that deed because he was the chosen one. God became doubtful again when Abraham touched his son's neck with his blade. Che vuoi? Isaac escaped because God became thoughtful enough to change his word at the last minute.

Both the shapeless and the human-shaped gods could create anxieties as complex as Himself. However, in a short while, the Jewish God transformed Himself into a Christian God. By that time, God had shifted His beliefs towards repenting and penances. God regretted the time He ordered the sacrifice of Abraham's son. To get out of that guilt, God sacrificed His only son for the Jews to kill. God's calculation was that they would let Immanuel off the hook after a few dramatic final moments, just like he saved Isaac. 'Che vuoi...' The anxious crowd was clueless about the expectations of God. They left the imprisoned one free and killed God's son. The son of God faced the helplessness of God with this question:

'My God, my God, why hast Thou forsaken me?'

To escape from the final question of His son, God screamed and asked another question of the followers of Abraham.

'Che volete... What are you expecting from me?'

The crowd became anxious again. They scattered, bearing a great guilt.

'Are you a Jew?'

That was Grusha's first question to Dora when she came back with a cup of tea.

'Whether I say yes or no, both will be false.'

Grusha looked at Dora with doubtful eyes. Dora offered the cup of tea without any change in her expression. As she took the cup, Grusha's face was filled with a disturbing anxiety.

'Do you know something? I am also a Jew... I am from Soviet Russia.'

'For me, the Soviet Union is the thick, smooth pages of a magazine. Papa used to cover all our schoolbooks with the thick sheets of that magazine. Once there was a picture of a worm on one of the sheets. Papa told me that it was a milk worm. I remember him explaining how it was born. In a big container, you have to keep fresh milk. In a few days, the milk will curdle and small worms will form in it. They will start eating each other in a while. After a while, there will be only three or four big worms. Eventually, one big worm will remain. Papa told us that it will then be cooked or fried. I still do not know if it is a real story or not. Yet, there is a cruel justice in deep-frying something that eats its own kind, isn't there?'

The question startled Grusha. She looked at Dora and wondered if the girl was talking nonsense or making fun of her after finding out the plans. Then she pretended to not understand Dora's question and shrugged her shoulders. About to sip the tea, she unknowingly searched for a milk worm in it. She felt like throwing up and changed the subject, fearing that Dora might start talking about milk worms again.

'I grew up in Russia until I turned thirteen. My papa was a gangster. After the decline of the Soviet Union, I fled to America with my mother. I had never practised religion until I became a teenager. I never felt I was a Jew while I was in the Soviet

Union. I always believed that my religion was communism. It was only after the decline of our nation that I found the Holy Torah in my papa's belongings. I realized my Jewishness only after reaching America. Anyway, only a refugee will display his identity in the strongest shades. The later years were those of doubts. Is it because God himself is perplexed, like you have mentioned in this article here?'

'Oh, I cannot say that I wrote it all on my own. Some of it is from what I read.'

'That is not my question. Whatever... There is a synagogue close by, right? Do you go there and pray?'

'No. In the synagogue here, there are no regular prayers any more. Even I have heard that this place was once filled with Jews. The holy migration to Israel started in the 1950s. Some of them are trying to migrate even now. But my allegiance is to the land I grew up in. Now there are only ten or thirteen Jewish families remaining here. Sometimes you wouldn't even find the sufficient number of people to conduct some prayers. The synagogue here is more of a museum than a place of worship. The people who enter it spend their time staring at the old clocks that have stopped working, the floor tiles, the peeling walls and the bell tower... They seldom pray. Even I go to the synagogue only to explain things to my visiting friends or foreign travellers. The only time I felt like praying was when the lovebirds I raised started dying from disease. When I need, I will find a rabbi myself who is attentive enough to listen to my sorrows and comfort me.'

Grusha wanted to continue the conversation. However, Lothar had returned by then. He parked his bike behind their house and came inside with a plastic packet in his hands. Dora went inside. Lothar opened the cover and took out six identical handguns.

'Lothar, I am taking these now. The money will reach you through Unni.'

'I know. Mustafa has told me everything.'

Arumukhan was bored. He was lighting another cigarette when his phone rang. It was Satheeshan. He said that Sheikh Musafir was under arrest and asked Arumukhan to get to the police station quickly. When he asked the driver to start the car, the driver turned away, pretending not to hear him. Arumukhan forcefully turned his face towards him by grabbing his chin and looked into his eyes.

'Can't you hear?' he asked.

The driver brushed away Arumukhan's hand and started the car.

Musafir was a regular visitor at the Ernakulam Public Library. That day, he was browsing through the new arrivals when he stumbled upon the childhood stories of the prime minister. After he read the blurb, he took the lighter out of his pocket and set the book on fire. Once it caught fire, he dropped it on the ground and stepped on it. When the librarian smelled smoke and rushed to the spot, Musafir was sitting on the floor, watching the book burn. The librarian came near Musafir and made a ruckus. Musafir pushed him back against a shelf full of books. The librarian fell, along with the books on the shelf. Musafir placed his foot on the librarian's chest and screamed madly.

'If I ever see this kind of book displayed here, I will burn you alive. Do you understand?'

He then ran to the reading room and sat down to calm himself.

Following the librarian's call, the police arrived within ten minutes and came to the reading room in search of Musafir. Head Constable Vasudevan approached Musafir and said, 'Bhai, there is a complaint. You need to come to the station.'

Musafir accompanied the policeman without another word.

When Arumukhan reached the station, Musafir was having a cup of tea with Head Constable Vasudevan. Arumukhan walked over to stand by Musafir.

'There he is, Sheikh's gambler. Do you know what he did today? I have heard stories about a Khalifa burning down the library of Alexandria. I don't even know if any of it is true. Anyway, today's event was something like that.'

Head Constable Vasudevan placed his teacup on the table. His whole body shook with laughter.

'Heard about it, sir. What can I say... Bhai is still in shock after Raul's death. He must have been high too. That is why...'

'I know, Arumukhan. The librarian called and complained. There was also a lot of pressure from Balakrishnan Nambiar. I couldn't ignore it. That is why I went there myself and brought him to the station. We haven't charged him yet. We have just kept him here until he cooled down. There is something rotten going on here. We can sense it. Call your advocate right away before anyone else calls from powerful places. Sheikh will have his medical reports with him, right? You can take him with you. Alright, Bhai, I will see you later.'

Arumukhan followed his advice. Musafir entered the car with Arumukhan.

'I left the foreigner *madamma* at Lothar's place in Mattancherry. If we don't get back there soon, she will panic.'

Arumukhan was right. When Grusha came out of Lothar's house with the plastic bag full of guns, she panicked when she couldn't find the car. Lothar recognized this and enquired. She told him the matter.

'They might have stepped out to get some tea or cigarettes. Let's wait for a while.'

Grusha nodded.

'You should remember one thing. These guns are empty. I will provide the bullets before the roulette. Anyway, we should meet that day, right?'

'Can I ask you something, Lothar? Why are you in this?'

'There should be some players in the game, right? You will be in trouble, otherwise. Do you know, I have made many guns. Yet I have never used any of them against anybody. I am tired of practising on empty bottles and wood stumps. In fact, I am tired of my life. I feel I must use the weapon I made at least once.'

Grusha wasn't sure that Lothar was telling the truth. She told Lothar that instead of waiting for the car, doing nothing, she would like to see the synagogue. She requested him to let Dora accompany her.

While walking towards Jew Street with Dora, she felt a mysterious ambience encircling her...the clean and empty streets, the metal figurines in the antique shops, the scent of incense and the red sky of the evening. She felt like dropping to the ground, crying out loud and repenting for her sins. Yet the dilapidated old doors on both sides of the street goaded her to continue walking. When she reached the synagogue, she clasped her hands on her stomach and prayed.

'Oh God, please take care of my child. I hid this even from Carl to avoid having to cancel this trip. Please help me complete this mission. Please grant me victory, even if it is a merciless one. *Ken y'hi ratzon...*' If it be Your will.

Grusha didn't realize how long she had been praying. When she opened her eyes, it was dark. She saw Dora coming out of an antique shop near the synagogue. Approaching Grusha, she started to walk faster.

'There is no need to hurry. I have a lot of time. Even if the car is back, they will wait for me.'

'When you came home, I told you that I was busy today. Don't you remember that?'

'Yes. Why are you busy?'

'There are two things. One, the assignment you looked at – it is almost over now. Second is a short story. I have to submit it for a cultural society's story competition. Tomorrow is the last date.'

'We need to walk for a while to reach home, right, Ruth? What is the story about? If you don't mind telling me...'

With the enthusiasm of finding her first reader, Dora started narrating her story.

'This is the story of a gangster. Someone from Kochi leaves the place in his youth and reaches Bombay. He joins a relative in Bombay, joins his gang and starts trading arms. He has a wife and two young daughters. One night, in a police encounter, his wife gets killed. He somehow escapes from the police with his daughters, leaves the city and returns to Kochi. In the city, even though they have his mother and his stepfather, they move away from them all and start a new life. This is how the story begins.'

'I like the beginning, Ruth. So, where are the gangster and the girls now?'

Dora continued the story, still not revealing their identities:

> The gangster came back to Kochi and started a workshop. During the day, he would be in the workshop, and all through the night, he would be in front of a piano under a dim light. Sola would listen to her drunken father at the piano. Dora would be busy trying to open the packets of sweets her papa brought.
>
> He called Sola to teach her how to play the piano, made her sit on his lap and started playing the black and white keys. To the tinkling rapid notes her father created, Sola would transform into a princess riding a wild horse. When the tune changed to something calm, Papa would be panting behind Sola, pressing his face into her hair and stroking it. When Sola removed his fingers from her hair and walked towards the kitchen to serve their dinner, she

would be shivering with fear. Since her whole attention was on the packet of sweets, Dora would be completely unaware of what had happened between them.

Whenever they were not in school, Dora and Sola would stay behind closed doors at home. Their papa took them out quite rarely. He believed that the police were still trying to hunt them down. He scared his daughters by telling them that someone would snatch them if they opened the doors or tried to step outside. Even so, they would escape into their father's uncle's shop and spend their time looking at the clothes of the passers-by. Their papa used to buy dark-coloured clothes for them. He would never take them to a textile shop to choose material for their frocks. Strangely enough, he never remembered to buy them undergarments. Sola used to station her sister Dora as a guard outside the school toilet whenever she went inside. Dora did not understand the need for this. But one day, when she had drifted away from her post as the guard, a bunch of girls entered the toilet and saw Sola in her papa's underwear. They made fun of her large underwear made for men and the period stain on it. When she listened to their taunts and saw her sister sobbing, Dora realized why the guard was necessary. She too cried along with her sister. That night, before Sola left for the kitchen after her regular piano session, she said, 'Papa, I need to buy underwear.'

Her papa lowered his eyes and agreed.

One day, Dora woke up early from her afternoon nap and ran outside, crying. It was a sacred day. She did not care about the heavy downpour. She ran to the antique shop near the synagogue and cried. The people there assumed that she might have had a fight with either her papa or Sola. They asked her why she was crying, and she told them, 'Nothing.' She couldn't understand whether what she had seen was a bad dream. She did not know how to answer those questions. The next day, Dora had a fever. She brushed away Sola's and Papa's hands whenever they came to check her fever. They left her alone.

She avoided their company. Closed doors. Hushed words. Feverish visions... Dora started wondering if she was living in a secret bunker. She spent her days with *The Diary of Anne Frank*. Her papa had brought it for her earlier. She would have believed it was her own writing had those been handwritten words instead of print.

Since she would have to cross the verandah to reach the toilet, she used to hold her pee in during nights. In her half-asleep state, she usually peed in her bed. In some time, she learned how to live alone in that house where all three of them lived.

Unni started frequenting their home to get guns for a lot of people in the city. One Onam, he gifted Dora and Sola new clothes. Dora got a brown frock, while Sola got a pale-yellow silk skirt. It was the first time in her memory that Sola had received a light-coloured piece of clothing. Even though she saw Sola hugging Unni in the piano room while their papa was not around, this time Dora did not feel afraid. She kept her head low and went inside her room. All the lovers of 'Pennunni' eventually became his whores. Yet his love for Solatido was pure. One day, he came, accompanied by the younger Arumukhan, and asked for her hand in marriage. Her papa called him a 'pimp' and pushed him out of their home.

Unni fixed a date for their wedding and informed Sola. Sola reached Unni's room the day before, but she refused to elope and get married to Unni. They argued. Unni took the half-empty beer bottle from which he was drinking, smashed it on her head and stabbed her in the stomach. She lay bleeding in his room the whole night. The police investigated the murder but to no avail. Yet when Unni read in the newspaper that Sola had been three months pregnant, he surrendered on his own to the police. Once he finished his six years of imprisonment, he came out, met Dora and begged for forgiveness.

Dora first met Getto when she went to pick up her computer's hard disk from his repair shop. After the bomb blast destroyed Simon's watch shop, Getto had established an electronics repair business in Kadavanthra. Dora had immediately noticed his name, which reminded her of the Warsaw ghetto, a detention centre for Jews during World War II. Upon picking up the repaired hard disk, she noticed Getto's narrow eyes and felt as though they conveyed a sense of disdain. For Getto, the hard disks he received to repair were a way to look into the memories and behaviour of people. When she realized it, she promised herself that she would never meet him again. Yet she couldn't keep the promise. She used to frequent the shop without even having a reason and would spend time talking to him. Even though her papa came to know about her relationship with Getto, he kept quiet. He had realized how his overt expressions of emotion had backfired in the case of his elder daughter. At night, when he played his piano drunkenly, he would seem like he was immersed in depression. Dora would go to her room and shut her door to avoid seeing him like that. She would dream about cockroaches infesting her body and would wake up, startled.

By the time Dora finished the story, they had reached Lothar's house. Dora hoped that her papa wouldn't be playing his piano when they got back. She hoped Grusha would never connect the story she had told to their life. The confused God betrayed her. When they reached the house, Lothar was playing the piano. Grusha realized she was looking into the face of the character she had heard about.

She was surprised to hear someone calling her by name in that strange street. Arumukhan and Musafir waved at her from across the street. She hurried towards the car, wanting to escape as fast as she could.

9

Donyi and Polo

Whoever met Getto often needed to change their plans – that's just how it was. When Dora left with the repaired hard disc, she had decided to never meet him again. Yet she was impelled to break that promise. She used to frequent his electronics shop whenever she got time; she loved his little nose and often kissed it playfully.

Everyone taking part in the roulette had to be met in person by Grusha as she had to explain to them the details about the financials, the rules and the way they should handle their weapons. It was Pandam Mustafa who informed Grusha that Getto was hiding in an antique shop at Mattancherry. Grusha immediately left for the place.

Grusha had noticed the antique shop the day before when she visited the synagogue. She had seen Dora coming out of that shop when she was at the synagogue. Dora hadn't informed anyone about Getto's presence there, not even Lothar. Dora didn't know that Grusha was here in this city to conduct a roulette in which her father and Getto were participating. She thought Grusha was some foreigner who wanted a gun for her own safety.

When Grusha reached the shop, an old man came to the door and invited her inside. Passing the shelves brimming with antique items, she reached the storage in the back. It was a dark room. The person who accompanied Grusha turned the lights on. In a corner of the dusty room, filled with old vessels and sculptures, Getto was eating. Startled at first, he smiled when he saw the old man. He washed his hands into the same plate from which he was eating and came up to Grusha. He shook hands with her. He hadn't wiped them after washing his hand.

When he touched Grusha's hand with his moist one, he remembered his mother...and his bedridden father. Getto had disclosed his personal stories only to Dora till now. He felt like confessing everything to her.

Gegong Tok, aka Getto, was from Arunachal Pradesh. He belonged to the Nyishi tribe. Dora now knew that 'Nyishi' in his language referred to the people. He lost both his parents at the time he was studying for a degree in electronics in Arunachal. He could not continue his education and left. He reached Kochi with his friend and neighbour, Ktodo. For a while, he and Ktodo worked as cooks in a Chinese restaurant. But before long, Getto got tired of the smells and the heat of the kitchen. His dreams were filled with soldering iron, small electronic components and circuit diagrams that resembled labyrinths.

By the time Getto learned to speak in broken Malayalam, Ktodo introduced him to Simon, Pandrand Albert's younger brother. After their father's death, the two brothers used to run the ironing shop. One day, a fight broke out in the neighbourhood after an argument about a church festival, and three people were stabbed. Simon was the main suspect. Simon escaped capture and fled to Lakshadweep, and from there he reached Colombo.

Maruthu from northern Sri Lanka taught him Tamil and how to repair watches. For Maruthu, the watch-repair shop was a front. Inside it, he made bombs for the Tamil Eelam Tigers. Simon became an apprentice to Maruthu. The case involving Simon dragged on for a while, but eventually the church committee decided not to pursue it. Simon returned to Kochi before the next year's festival. He took a shop for lease near the cemetery and started his watch-repair shop in the bigger room. He sublet the smaller room for Saraswatiyamma to run her flower shop. Simon's shop slowly picked up. He carefully attended to all the orders he received. He also made local bombs secretly. But there weren't many takers for local bombs those days.

When Getto joined Simon, the first thing he noticed was his bare wrists. He repaired everyone's watches, but Getto never saw him wear one. Getto used to smile whenever Simon went out and asked passers-by for the time. The day Simon and Albert died in a bomb blast, Getto was stuck in the hospital. He was accompanying his friend Ktodo's sister Reyo, who was running a high fever. The younger Arumukhan came and informed him about the death of Simon and Albert. When Reyo held on to his hands and started talking gibberish, Getto felt that Simon's ghost was talking to him through her.

After Simon's death, Getto worked as an illegal contract worker in some IT firms. Since he had not completed his graduation, there was no scope for a real job anywhere for him. Getto sold off his home in Arunachal, and with that money, he started his electronics shop in Kadavanthra. At first, he used to repair radios, televisions and electric irons. Later it progressed to a computer hardware maintenance shop. That was where he met Dora. She used to come over whenever he was not busy. One such days, inside the locked shop, he rested his head on her lap and narrated his story. Dora realized that while doing so, he assumed a poetic, literary language, and she would listen, caressing his hair.

Getto's father was a part of Arunachal's police force. He was a tough man. Almost all of Getto's childhood memories began with a scene where his drunk father was beating up his mother. Most days he would be drunk on the local brew, apong. Immediately after he stepped into the home, he would beat his wife up for silly reasons. Getto's mother was a wise woman. Still, she subjected herself to this torture and lived with her husband. Since she knew that he would become more violent if she resisted, she would lie still and simply sob. It sounded like a squeaking pulley or a chalk screeching while drawing a line on the blackboard. Once he was satisfied, his father would push her out of the bed. Getto would often feel as if he had recovered a precious lost object when she came away to him.

Getto was her only solace. Having satisfied his father's bestiality, his mother would roll off his bed and get into Getto's, hug him and kiss him on his forehead. When her tears flowed over his forehead, he would wipe them off with the blanket. He often felt as if his mother was a sieve from which many fluids gushed out. His father's drunken smell would engulf him through his mother. To get over that, he used to kiss her on her lips over and over. Eventually his father's stench would vanish.

Tears on his forehead...

Blood from the wounds his father would make...

Sweat on her palm...

Spit, sweat and semen from his father...

At that moment, his mother was a liquid being.

His father got transferred to Itanagar when Getto was thirteen. Even though Getto's father had never been away from the family, he left for Itanagar without them. Slowly he became a nuisance that could be ignored when it presented itself for a day or two each month. It was only then that he started to see a smile on his mother's face.

She used to wear the customary loose dress Nyishi women wore. It was secured at the waist with a thread hidden under metal ornaments. Her hair would always be parted in the middle and tied up neatly in a bun at the nape of her neck. A brass necklace adorned her always, a small bell attached to it. She used to wear sandals only when she went out. Getto remembered everything about her. When his father moved out of their home, nobody occupied his bed. Even when her mother insisted, he refused. He was afraid he would turn out to be a cruel man if he started sleeping in his father's bed.

Getto was in the second year of college when his father was attacked by Naga rebels. Injured in the head, he lost his memory and eventually his job. His paralyzed father occupied the bed in the house once again. For the first two or three days after his father's return, Getto felt a surge of anger. But what was the point of being angry at a man who was completely paralysed and had no memory? His anger turned to pity. Getto's mother would roll over to his father's side at night, undress herself and try to wake him up. When she realized that he wouldn't move, she went back to sleep.

One night, she murmured to Getto, 'Your father is crying. I think he is worrying about something...'

Getto thought that his mother was lying. His father had no memory, and he wouldn't even feel pain if you cut him. There was no way his father would cry. His mother then touched him with her fingers wet with his father's tears. Getto was learning about a new liquid other than blood, spit and semen through his mother. His father's tears. He recognized the burning heat of his father's tears on his cheeks. Before the tears could burn his face, he wiped them off. He stood up, turned the lights on and went near his father. His father lay there, shedding tears. When Getto realized that all the world's pain lay condensed in that sight, he sat on the floor. Getto closed his eyes and cried like he used to on those nights when his father unleashed his violence on his mother.

Getto had constantly tried to jog his father's memory, looking for some response, but in vain. Then his father offered some hope in the form of his tears – the day before his mother committed suicide. After her death, there was not even that. If he had responded in any way, Getto could have had his revenge. He even contemplated poisoning his father. Yet, he couldn't act on those thoughts. A year and a half after his mother's death, Getto's father also died.

Maybe it was his failure to retrieve his father's memory that drove him towards retrieving computer memories. He replenished those digital body parts in the best possible ways. That was why Getto charged less than the other repair places in the city.

For him, every device with a severed memory represented his father. In that body where even the burning-hot soldering iron cannot produce a movement, the soldering flux burst like smallpox bubbles. The flesh melted in that heat, and the bones were exposed like the legs of an electronic chip. Every device he repaired was his vengeance against his father. It saved him from the pity he felt towards his father in his final days.

By the time he finished his story, Getto was panting. His face burned like a soldering iron. Realizing that, Dora kissed him. His hands searched around her body as if he was searching for himself. He begged Donyi and Polo, Mother Sun and Father Moon, for forgiveness. His tribal beliefs taught him that there was a soul for everything under the sun and the moon, from trees and flowers to the land and mountain. Yet he had ignored that rule when it came to his father.

After his mother's death, he stopped his studies midway. After that year's Nyokum Yullo festival that February, he left for Kochi. In the data-entry job he had with an IT company before setting up his own shop, Getto was distressed by the multiple shifts the job entailed. He hated the idea that someone else would occupy the chair and the space he left behind after his shift. He detested it when things and places did not have a single person to control them. To fix that space as his own, he left his dandruff flakes all over the keyboard, yet he was terrified when he left his seat.

He started to find bigger happiness in the smaller things around him. He invented reasons to arrive at such happy moments. The day when he ate something he liked, the day when he pooped well, the day when he watched a good movie, the day when he took a longer time to come while masturbating, the day when he rejuvenated the memory discs that he thought would never come alive, the day when unexpectedly he spent less money...and so on.

Ktodo's sister Reyo used to sell woollen clothes near Subhash Park. She resembled a little lamb. Getto often asked himself why he never fell for her even after she had shown interest in him. One evening, while haggling, someone grabbed her. Reyo spat on his face. Undeterred, he hugged her and kissed her in public, got on a bike that was parked nearby and drove off. Reyo had noticed him visiting the park often. He used to stand near the cigarette shop and smoke or chew paan. Whenever he glanced towards her, she would angrily spit on the floor. At times, he had passed by, touched her woollen goods, glanced at her breasts, uttered 'How smooth' and disappeared into the park.

The day after the incident, Ktodo and Getto waited for him in the park. When he entered the park, Reyo signalled them. Ktodo was the first to start the fight. Getto joined him. The policeman on duty intervened. The man pushed the policeman aside and started beating Ktodo and Getto. Reyo screamed. When the city patrolling group got the policeman's message, a police jeep arrived and took the three of them to the station. In less than an hour, Pandam Mustafa arrived with an advocate. The man whom Ktodo and Getto had tried to beat up was a member of Mustafa's gang. Escorting him from the station, Mustafa turned back and looked at them several times. The police charged Ktodo and Getto with disturbing the peace. By the time they got out after pleading in the court, Mustafa's men had destroyed Getto's electronics shop. The next evening, Getto reached a bar Mustafa frequented. He grabbed Mustafa by the collar and pulled him down to the floor. He was about to stab Mustafa with the small knife he had hidden in his waistband when Mustafa's friends caught hold of him and beat him up. When he regained consciousness, he was in the police lock-up.

It was Unni who got Getto out of the police station. By the time they reached Musafir's place, Getto had explained everything to Unni in his broken Malayalam.

'No fucker will touch you now, all right?' Unni pacified him.

When they reached Musafir's place, Musafir was asleep. Unni woke him up.

'Bhai, this is the guy who tried to attack Mustafa yesterday and got arrested. We must save this guy.'

'Let Raul come. I will tell him,' Musafir mumbled in his sleep.

That day, when Raul returned, he brought Satheeshan with him. Getto and Satheeshan joined the gang on the same day. Getto would never forget that day. Because it was the day they found Reyo's body under the North railway bridge, raped and killed.

Even though Ktodo went back to Arunachal after his sister's death, Getto didn't return. Getto became friends with Unni. Eventually he became a trusted member of the gang. Yet when Satheeshan saved Raul's life, he gained the upper hand in the gang. Getto started distancing himself from Raul.

After offering his wet hand to Grusha at the antique shop, he immediately withdrew his hand and apologized. Grusha didn't seem to mind and smiled at him.

'Is it true that you betrayed Raul?'

'Not me. One thing is true: I had some issues with the gang. But I would never betray Raul. Even Musafir Bhai knows it well. I had contacted Bhai. It was Musafir Bhai who asked me to hide until the roulette. Bhai told me that whoever remains in the roulette will replace Raul in the gang. I will be participating in the roulette representing our gang.'

Once Getto confirmed it, the final list of players for the roulette was ready in Grusha's mind. She bid him goodbye and left. After she got into the car, she contacted Unni. He had agreed to find a place to hold the roulette. She had mentally prepared herself to be the conductor of the roulette. She felt like entering the synagogue to pray. But one of Carl's jokes boomed inside her: that gods are the cruellest gangsters in history and their members have been engaged in a gang war for centuries. While her car moved through roads shimmering in the midday heat, Grusha tried to take comfort in the fact that she was no longer passing through the mystical atmosphere she had experienced the day before.

10

Scribbles

Dear Carl,

I am scared, to tell you the truth. I feel like dropping everything and going back. I can't get over the feeling that the companies have sent me here to do something utterly wrong. Why would our company decide on this way to conduct the competition? There are no satisfying answers. I don't have much of an idea about the other company participating. Since all the details are confidential, I know nothing about them beyond an email id. Yet, they are giving me timely instructions and responses to each mail I send. Do you know anything about the second company? Balakrishnan Nambiar – he seems to be controlling everything. Which company is he representing? Or is he just a middleman? Or is this roulette his idea?

I have met everyone participating in the roulette except Mustafa, who is playing hide-and-seek with me. He is still an unknown entity. The rest of them are probably reconciled to die.

I don't know what will happen or how things will resolve. I am really scared, Carl. I have kept six guns for the death bet. The guns were made by someone named Lothar, who incidentally plays the piano very well. He has a daughter, a Jewish beauty. But you cannot make fun of her using your regular Jewish jokes because her nose is not as long as mine.

Yet, those guns... Even though there are no bullets, after I had them in my room, I couldn't sleep. I am sure that a bullet is waiting for me too. We know people who keep a gun under their pillow and sleep peacefully. Yet even empty guns are nibbling away at my peace here.

Lothar playing roulette is going to be his daughter's chance to escape from that house, which resembles a closed cave. You have heard the news of Raul's death. It has shaken the gang completely. The arguments to decide the next leader are getting intense. I think Getto and Satheeshan are taking part in this roulette to fix that. For Satheeshan, this is a continuation of his dreams. He is ready to go to any extent for this.

Getto isn't participating in this just to become the leader of the gang. Some believe that Getto betrayed Raul. This is the only way to prove his allegiance to the gang. If not, his own gang members would shoot him down. Not just that, this is his one chance to get rid of Lothar and make Dora (Lothar's daughter, Ruth) his own. Sort of like ancient tribal justice...

Most of the gang members are supporting Satheeshan, including the poor old Arumukhan.

I sense that Unni will support Getto. He is the businessman and pimp of this city. He advertises a 'friendship network' to provide male and female escorts to those who want it. He is buying over the city as the proxy for someone. This would be yet another match fixed by him in advance.

I had mentioned that policeman, right? I was scared of him when I heard about him. What you say is true. Your preconceptions are often wrong. Bappu is like a snake that has lost its venom. He is too old to catch prey or move away. Yet he will hiss at times to prove to himself that he can still bite. This roulette might be like euthanasia for Bappu. What I do not seem to understand is Sheikh Musafir and his reasons to join this roulette. He is the only confusing figure for me. Why am I reminded of my papa whenever I think about him?

Carl, all that I told you about me is not true. My papa was not a gangster. He was not nicknamed Dragon. My papa was a poor artist. He was a Russian who took part in a roulette once and got shot in the first round itself. Carl, I am scared. Damn it, aren't you back from your vacation in Las Vegas yet? Can't you send me some jokes to overcome these fears? Let me share some Russian jokes with you for now.

'My grandfather had taken part in that,' a student said aloud in class while talking about the Russian civil war. The teacher asked her to bring her grandfather the next day and introduce him to the class. Next day her grandfather came to the class. The children came to him. They asked, 'Tell us, Grandpa, have you met the revolutionary leader Chapayev?'

'I have seen him with these two eyes of mine.'

'Where did you meet the brave Chapayev?'

'I was near a river, cleaning my uniform. That was when I saw him swimming with such vigour. My comrades next to me asked me to shoot him. I grabbed my gun and shot him dead. I met Chapayev for the first time when I was aiming that shot.'

The student turned to her friends and proudly said, 'Didn't I tell you that my grandpa has taken part in the civil war?'

Carl, I think I am going to get the role of that grandpa in this roulette.

While grazing sheep in the forest, a Russian shepherd and his four or five sheep fell into a pit. Since the pit was quite deep, they couldn't escape. Listening to the bleats of the sheep, a wolf also came running and fell into the same pit. The sheep started crying frantically, but the shepherd was calm. He said, 'The wolf knows whom to eat first. I am safe here. My only fear is that I won't be able to escape before he finishes all the sheep.'

I know that Russian roulette is a pit like this. Since the sheep are with me, it will take a little while for the wolf to get to me. That is all. I need to prepare my foothold on the side of the pit with the help of my crook. This damned roulette! Why am I not ending my journey towards it myself? I am tired. I wish to give up all this and return to you, I really do.

Carl, I know this is a long mail. You know, I always send long emails when I am scared. I hope you will respond soon.

With love,
Grusha.

Dear Grusha,

I got back from my vacation yesterday. Las Vegas was quite an experience. Since I was alternating between drinks and the casino, I was in no state to write to you. Sorry about that. Yet I spent all my time thinking about how exciting and dangerous this death bet is, which you are planning in that city, much more than all the games I played in the casinos. I see that you are curious about the second company taking part in the bet. Before I tell you about it, you need to know a few more things.

Do you know why I started sending cyber jokes to you? You know that you haven't told me about your Jewish ethnicity, not even once. Then why would I send you emails to offend your ethnicity? You should have realized right then that I know all about you. But like any girl in love, you started acting stupidly. The company needed to get you to run this roulette somehow. It was the company's decision that I fall in love with you and get you to do its bidding. I am just a loyal servant.

I do not have a clear picture about what is happening in that city. I don't have any problems in sharing what I know – or what I assume to be true.

There is no second company... There is only one company that is interested in that disputed land, and for that purpose they have set up yet another shell company to get control of that city. We need the help of the government and police to do that. Getting rid of the criminals there is a first step to achieve that. This roulette is a secret agreement between our company and their government and police. I have also wondered, like you, about the role our company has in all this. Grusha, it is completely possible that our company also got caught up in this business. Under the guise of setting up a shell company, all this may have already been planned by someone we don't know. I am not sure about that. We cannot guess everything. I am only sure about the certain result – deaths.

In fact, this Russian roulette is a betrayal. Nobody can predict how the world outside will hear about this when it is over. Perhaps the media will report it as a gang war. The gangs in that city are destined to kill and get killed. Perhaps it will be portrayed as an encounter with the police. If yes, what is going to happen is merely a rehearsal for many other such incidents all over the city. You must not expect them to act foolishly and remove all the gangsters all at once since even they do not know who will replace them. I sure don't know what they are up to.

There is yet another possibility. After the leaders of all the gangs are removed, the police, the middlemen or the companies will control the gangs. I am telling you this at the very last hour, but this is a play that has been in the making for a while now. The company is introducing you as an actor who will appear only in the last scene. So please finish your role and return to the green room as soon as you can. In the dim light, remove your makeup. Get out immediately. You do not get to stay back to find out how the story ends or whether it entertains the viewers or bores them. It will happen in the way it has been decided.

I am telling you all this not because I am in love with you or because I am feeling guilty. I am informing you on the company's instructions. The company is insistent that you should understand all this at least two days before the roulette. Even if you know all the details, you will not be able to wear the hat of a traitor now – I mean, you cannot change anything even if you want to. If you behave like that, the company will not be responsible for any of your actions and their consequences. It is only wise to realize that the trap you have set on behalf of the company has entrapped you too. It has already been decided who will kill, who will die, who will get caught and who will watch this game that we play. If you try to ignore my warning and try to act independently, it will be utterly foolish. Grusha, her papa and her mamma will just be three people who died in the riots after the Soviet Union fell. The twenty-nine years you lived after that will merely be a bonus the company granted to you. I cannot even tell you to 'decide what you want'. The company, along with others, has already decided what all our decisions should be. I know you will be even more terrified reading all this.

Here are the jokes you asked for...

A Jewish man was anxiously twisting and turning in his bed, unable to sleep. His wife asked, 'What is bothering you?'

'I had told our neighbour that tomorrow I would return the money I borrowed from him. I don't have a penny.'

His wife opened the door, stepped out and yelled at the neighbour. 'My husband will not return the money he borrowed from you – not tomorrow, not ever.'

She returned and told her husband, 'Now you can sleep peacefully. The neighbour will lose his sleep until we return his money.'

You shouldn't lose your sleep and be scared. The job entrusted to you is to make others lose their sleep. Here's another one.

An officer told the Jew who had decided to shift permanently to America, 'In your application, it is shown that you do not have any relatives abroad. But it is also stated that your brother is in Israel.'

'What I told you is true. My brother is in his country. I am the one who has come abroad.'

Grusha, it is important whom you are loyal towards. You will be safe so long as your allegiance is towards the company.

A Jew talking to another Jew who is reading an Arabic newspaper: 'Are you crazy? Why are you reading the newspaper of Arabs?'

'My friend, I read a Jewish newspaper regularly. What is there in it? Jews are getting victimized, Palestine is attacking Israel, Jews all over have lost their wealth and their peace of mind. You take a look at the headlines of this Arab newspaper. Jews are controlling the most important banks in the world, Jews are at the top of the world media, Israel is defeating Palestine using their huge arms resources. Shouldn't we be reading news that brings us joy?'

We must give utmost importance to our peace and happiness, whatever the situation. If you don't understand that, you are a fool. Our safety depends on the stand we take. It is our responsibility to ensure our own safety.

It was the time of the Cold War between Russia and America. This was how an American senator responded to the success of the Russian space mission:

'This is not a big deal. The only conclusion from this is that their Jews are better than our Jews. That's all.'

You shouldn't bother so much about the two major gangs in the city or about their lives. You should only view this as a bet to find out the best among the two.

I am sure that none of these Jew jokes will ease your fears. Yet you need to complete the task that the company has entrusted you with. You must keep all these details confidential. Otherwise, guns which you have purchased for the roulette will turn against you.

Bappu, the middleman between the police and the gangs.

Musafir, who might or might not be crazy.

Arumukhan, the poor soul who is more like the joker in a stack of cards.

Mustafa, whom you haven't met yet.

Satheeshan, who would dare to do anything to become the leader.

Getto, who has transformed into a hot soldering iron.

Lothar, who gave you the weapons.

Unni, who is pimping the city out.

And many others you do not know.

Balakrishnan Nambiar, who is tying all of them to the shell company.

Are you sure one among them might not kill you for the company? If you think they won't, you are the shepherd who has fallen into the hole. By the time you discover that all the sheep you reserved for the cruel wolf are actually wolves in sheep's clothing, even death cannot show kindness to you. I am telling you this because of a little bit of love I felt towards you at some point. The only option left for you is to return after completing the roulette as soon as possible.

With love,
C.W.

Carl,

I had my doubts whether the company was aiming for a gang war when I learnt of the changes they suggested for the rules of the roulette. But I am realizing the extent of the danger only now. I am not shocked any more, but I am disgusted that I assisted them in this betrayal. I am sure that this roulette is going to create an explosion in this city. It will be well if you all remember one thing: nobody can escape from the repercussions of this event. Let me share another Russian joke.

After the nuclear disaster at Chernobyl, reports came out that the mushrooms growing there carried hazardous content. Someone asked an old woman who was selling mushrooms by the side of the road, 'What are you doing here? Will anyone buy these poisonous mushrooms now?'

'Why not? As long as there are cruel superiors and loveless couples in the world, my sales will always remain unaffected.'

To commemorate the victory here, I will throw a party once I am back. I will serve Russian delicacies that you have never tasted before. I will serve Molotov cocktails and Chernobyl mushrooms for you and our superiors.

Grusha

Dear Grusha,

A lion, a bear and a boar were getting ready for a game of cards. Before they started their game, the lion warned them all. 'If any of you cheat in the game, I will scratch your nose off. If you try to leave midway, I will chew on your fat meat.'

This is a match where the results are already fixed. This is a gamblers' boar hunt. Understand that there is no way the hunted will escape.

Regards,

C.W.

Carl,

I had kept an important piece of news from you. Now you are never going to know what it was.

Grusha.

Grusha,

Are you referring to the news of your pregnancy? Did you forget that there are no secrets for anyone in this world? The company and I found out about all that through the medical check-up they did before sending you to India.

My belated congratulations.

C.W.

As Grusha caressed her belly, for a moment she felt like Mary, in Dora's story, who berated God.

11

The Day Before

Grusha woke up when the alarm rang on her mobile phone. She had a bad hangover. She had resumed drinking yesterday, after giving it up when she had first learned that she was pregnant. Arumukhan gave her company. The whole night, Arumukhan remained outside Grusha's hotel room, guarding her like a watchdog. Even though Musafir had sent him to watch over her, Grusha couldn't help wondering if he was also a spy. After reading the emails sent by Carl, she feared and suspected everyone.

She remembered speaking to Arumukhan ceaselessly. She spoke about her papa who lost his life in a game of roulette, her mother who was forced to leave her country, about herself and how she grew up bewildered and scared, about her cheater boyfriend, about the companies that betray everyone... Arumukhan merely smiled at her when she spoke to him in a language he failed to comprehend. He felt that Grusha looked like the queen in a deck of cards, who have a head on top, whichever way you throw it. He took out his deck of cards from his pocket. They played rummy late into the night. Grusha kept losing. Arumukhan refused to lose even to get Grusha interested in the game. She stopped the game after getting tired of losing constantly. She threw the cards, walked towards the cupboard, and aimed a gun at Arumukhan. He jumped up, frightened, and yelled. The cards fell all over the floor. He shivered in fear, shook his head and cried. Grusha shot the gun over and over without bullets. Both of them laughed.

Grusha handed over the gun to Arumukhan, went closer, stood behind him and aimed at the image reflected in the mirror. After many years as a part of the gang, it was the first time he was touching a gun. Grusha practised shooting by holding on to his fingers, Arumukhan panicking at each empty click. Grusha moved closer to him. She thought she smelled the larch trees of her childhood. When she felt a shooting pain in her stomach, she threw the gun on the bed and caressed her belly. She whimpered and imagined herself as the queen from the cards, with two heads and no belly. When the clueless Arumukhan tried to console her, she pushed him outside and locked herself in.

Arumukhan stood alone in the hotel corridor with its dim light. He had already heard about the bet from Musafir. It disturbed him no end – all those lives hanging on a chance. He spent the rest of the night walking along the dimly lit corridor. Grusha woke up from her sleep many times, riddled with the same nightmare. She was sitting with Carl Walker and the CEO on top of a big tree. The CEO was holding a gun. Carl had a metal rod. Grusha was holding a torch light. Under the tree, many dogs were waiting, dogs with human heads. All of them were searching for a wild boar that might grunt and arrive any moment. Tired of waiting, when she slowly drifted off to sleep on top of the tree, her alarm rang and she woke up.

She pressed her fingers into her forehead and walked into the bathroom. She stood under the shower and slowly rubbed her belly and closed her eyes. She came out, dressed quickly and picked up her bag to go out. Arumukhan was sleeping outside, his head resting on a flower pot. She woke him up. He got up and went inside the room to wash his face. Then he picked up the cards that were scattered all over the floor and the bed, put them back into his pocket and came out. By the time they locked the room and reached downstairs, their driver was waiting for them near the reception. She directed the driver to take them to Sheikh Musafir's place.

When they reached Musafir's house, he was talking to another gang member. When he saw them, he folded the newspaper in his hands, put it aside and walked towards them. Grusha smiled with bright eyes at Musafir, who was bare-chested and wearing a lungi. Musafir invited them in, but Grusha affectionately refused.

'Why would we sit here and waste our time? I feel like roaming around the city the whole day today.'

'I will come with you right away. You don't have a problem if Arumukhan joins us, right?'

Grusha shook her head. Musafir came back, wearing a loose half-sleeved shirt and faded jeans.

Grusha shared the front seat with the driver. Kochi was just waking up from slumber in the mild morning sun. They drove through the streets, which soon started buzzing with people.

Nobody spoke inside the car. They had fixed their eyes on the people outside. Grusha became restless when the silence inside the car became unbearable for her.

'Musafir, five years back, when I reached India for the first time, it was not this crowded. Kochi is growing in all respects.'

'Everyone talks about how Kochi is growing. Grusha, these are just peripheral changes. She may be growing taller, but she is not expanding. If you go back eight or ten years, can you find buildings as tall as these? From a little girl, she has become taller. Yet the expanse of the city is the same. That is why we have this crowd here. Now she is a woman wearing a tight dress belonging to a little girl. People get attracted to her fetishist look. Those who have inhabited this place for years know that the city is actually shrinking. She will shrink and shrink, and one day she will suffocate all of us. Still, people will wait for their turn to get a space in this crowd. She would still be like a whore, lying down lasciviously at the shore of the Arabian Sea. There will be a mysterious smile on her lips. To make that smile brighter, the sea and the lake will join, and wet her lips with saliva. It will be a smile people will kill for.'

'Nice... That's so poetic, Sheikh.'

'It is not like that... I can only talk like this about this city.'

'I am not going to argue with you.'

'How can you escape like that? You are here to settle all disputes in a single sweep, right? For you, isn't this city just a betting place?'

Grusha's face darkened. To deviate from the topic, she asked about the places Musafir liked to go in the city and suggested that they go to all those places. He was startled, like a man awaiting death sentence who is suddenly asked his last wish. When they were near the Durbar Hall, Musafir asked the driver to stop. He jumped out of the car and walked into the art gallery to join the people who were there to see an art exhibition. After the car was parked by the side of the road, Grusha joined him to watch the exhibition. Arumukhan also went in with her, but he was quickly bored and stepped out to light a cigarette.

As he stepped out of the art gallery, Musafir told Grusha that he was very hungry. She instructed the driver to go to a restaurant. Musafir ordered Malabari dum biryani for lunch. When the fragrant biryani arrived in its clay pot, Musafir tried to remember his mother. The scent of biryani was the only thing that took him back to the home he came from. After reaching Kochi, he hadn't visited Malappuram even once. When his mother passed away, Musafir had been in prison. He came to know about his father's death one week after it happened. Grusha observed her three companions, who had kept their knives and forks aside and were eating the biryani with their fingers. She tried to imitate them but returned to her knife and fork after wiping the ghee from the biryani on a paper towel. Musafir noticed that and started teasing her.

'Grusha, we don't keep weapons with us when we eat food or when we pray. Do you know anyone else like that?'

'I know someone like that.'

'Who?'

'Yasser Arafat...the famous Palestinian leader... He followed the same rules as you when it came to weapons.'

Musafir looked at her and smiled. She found her peace in that smile in the same way the jokes comforted her.

'If I ask you something, not on behalf of the company, will you give me an answer?' she asked.

'Are you going to ask why a few of us continue to live like this?'

Grusha nodded.

'The street dancer told the Buddhist monk when he walked away after seeing her dance, "You became a monk by suppressing your desire to dance." The monk agreed, but do you know what his reply was? That what she said was completely true. But she too was dancing by suppressing her desire to become a monk. Here, too, things are that simple. Who doesn't like to break the rules and live? There will always be a few people who would not repress their desires.'

Grusha did not respond.

'Did you finish meeting all those whom you wanted to meet?' Musafir asked.

'No. Mustafa hasn't met me. I have only very little knowledge about him.'

'I remembered this when you talked about him. Last week, when I was in the hospital, on a day of a hartal – that means a protest – something funny occurred. Two medical-shop owners were fighting with each other near Jose Junction. On the day of the hartal, both the shop owners paid Mustafa to destroy the other's shop. Mustafa accepted both offers. On the day of the hartal, he got hold of a few kids and a few political banners and destroyed both the shops. He even took money from both the parties. In Kochi, such games are rampant now.'

'Do you know anything more about him?'

'There is nothing really to talk about him. He is just an odd boy who spent his time on liquor and ganja around Palarivattom and Thammanam. When there was no more money left, he would fight it out. When that didn't work any more, he started roaming around in the city with a knife, collecting tens and twenties from the shop owners. They often gave him money to avoid a nuisance in front of their shops. When it became a habit, one shopkeeper picked a quarrel with him. Mustafa slashed him inside his own shop.

'When Mustafa came out from jail after sorting out the case against him, people started fearing him. He started his career as a thug for a Marwari who lent money against gold jewellery. That is how he got the name "Pandam" Mustafa – pandam means gold jewellery. Later he had disagreements with the Marwari. Some politicians asked him to handle their affairs, and he started to grow. With the help of the politicians, he got hold of a few people in the police force, and eventually he subsumed all the small gangs in Kochi. Crime in Kochi became synonymous with Mustafa. Eventually, when he became a disgrace to the party, the local politicians stopped associating with him publicly. With that, he left the parties in Kerala and became the leader of some north Indian party which had no influence in any of these areas. It is said that he is now on a spiritual path. The story goes that he plans crimes all day and goes to the mosque in the evening, where he prays and cleans the floor of the mosque as a penance. This city never falls short of stories. He always had an issue with our gang. Not just that...we have an old account to settle.'

Musafir rubbed an old wound on his leg and fell silent. Grusha's mobile rang. It was a call from Balakrishnan Nambiar. He informed her that there was an urgent company email and she should look at it immediately. He also informed her that Unni would call her soon, and then he disconnected the call. Grusha opened her mailbox. There were just two lines in the email.

The place is decided. You will be informed shortly.

'How are Mustafa and Unni connected to this Nambiar?'

'The story goes back some eight years. Nambiar had a petrol pump in his wife's name on the Angamaly highway. One night, there was a police raid based on a complaint that they were selling adulterated petrol. His competitors thought they could trap Nambiar like that. They also planned their deals accordingly. But you know how business works... If you make a mistake, then it becomes the weak link in the chain that keeps breaking. Since Nambiar knew this well, he tried to spend a lot of money and settle it with the people who came for the raid. The officers refused to budge and slapped a case on him. That was when Nambiar started his relationship with Mustafa, when he asked him to fix the problem of the officers. The next day, the newspapers carried the news that four or five people died while driving drunk and crashing into a petrol pump. It was those officers.'

'What about Unni?'

'Young girls are Nambiar's weakness. Unni will not hesitate to pimp out his own wife if he can make a profit from it.'

After dropping off the others at their places, Grusha and Musafir reached his house. She got out of the car and followed him. Grusha asked, almost as an afterthought, 'Could you step back from all this, Musafir? This roulette is a trap to finish all of you.'

'It is sheer luck that you did not say this inside the car. If you did that, you wouldn't have reached your hotel. Beware of your driver. Even though he is under suspension now, he is a policeman. Not just a common policeman – he is a policeman goon. Our Balakrishnan Nambiar's youngest daughter is a rotten egg. She had a sexcapade with some guy for a few days, and the guy did something nasty. Somehow, a pornographic cassette of the girl became a hot-selling item in Kochi. When Nambiar came to know this, he unleashed the police all over Kochi, and in a matter of two days, all the videocassette libraries here were raided. They confiscated that cassette alone. There was a boy running a video library near Getto's shop. He hid a copy, and when the mayhem of police raids ended, he released the cassette again. Your driver was the superintendent's gunman at the time. One day, he walked into that shop and shot that boy down. It was recorded in the court that while the policeman was browsing for a cassette, the shopkeeper tried to touch the policeman's gun and shot himself by accident. Getto was the only witness to the event. He was not part of the gang then. Nambiar and Unni made sure that he kept his mouth shut. Since there were no other witnesses, the case didn't stand. Bappu was the one who arranged this driver for Balakrishnan Nambiar. So, let it be! What I was saying was... Grusha, I have no choice but to participate in this death bet. I have spent countless nights waiting for this moment, feigned madness and, at times, pretended to be completely insane.'

Musafir smiled. Grusha returned to the car. She was more terrified of the driver now than of the dragon. She glanced at Musafir going into his home and closed her eyes.

When the car was near Marine Drive, Grusha received a call from Unni. He told her that he had a godown – a storehouse – near a place called Pathalam. He said that Nambiar would come and meet her soon with all the details and asked her to hand over the phone to the driver. After finishing the conversation with Unni, the driver parked the car by the side and got out. By the time he finished chewing on his paan masala, Balakrishnan Nambiar's car reached the other side of the road. Nambiar was driving and was alone. Grusha's driver crossed the road and went to Nambiar. He handed over a sealed envelope to the driver and waved at Grusha. She waved back. By the time she opened the envelope, Nambiar's car had disappeared.

Grusha asked the driver to park the car someplace where it was not crowded. She sat on an empty bench and stared at a puddle. She remembered something and took out the phone from her pocket to make a call.

'Hello, Mamma... Yes, I am well... You should be ready. I'll be there in another four days. We will go on a trip... Hey, no no. This will be a long trip – outside the States... What? To Russia? Hey, not sure. Maybe it is also possible. I haven't decided yet... I have emailed Uncle Alan to get everything ready for us. You should call him and remind him. I don't have to tell you about his memory, right? Mamma, get everything ready. I'll be back soon. Bye, now.'

Grusha sat there till sundown. When she returned to the car, her face was calm.

Grusha reached the hotel. Arumukhan was ready for his usual guard duty and was sitting in the visitor's lounge. She told the reception manager that she didn't need company and directed him to send Arumukhan back. She went to her room, removed her clothes and lay down. When she placed her laptop on her stomach, the little life inside her protested, and she moved the laptop down to her thighs. She felt as if there was a spy built inside her to take notice of all her movements. She had expected to see an email from Carl when she opened her inbox. But there was nothing except the official emails.

After the second-show movie, Arumukhan sat at Pai Dosa Shop and fiddled with the food before him, unable to eat. When he got tired of that, he paid the bill and left. He got into an autorickshaw passing by and took out his deck of cards. When he failed to decipher the numbers and the signs on the cards in the dark, he started throwing them out one by one. By the time he finished the last card in the deck, he had reached Musafir's house.

Musafir was mumbling like a mad man and was smoking a joint.

'Who will I shoot first tomorrow amongst you guys?

'Bappu, I haven't forgotten the curses and cries of Pandrand Albert. I haven't forgotten the lies you spewed in front of Judge Fakir Mohamed. Don't you remember those who suffered your brutality?

'Mustafa, even if the wound in my leg heals, the one in my heart will remain. Do you know how long I have waited for a duel with you?

'Lothar...we do not have anything between us. Why do you come to my gunpoint then?

'Satheeshan, Getto, my kids... My gun will aim at one of you first tomorrow. How long will I continue as a mere minister for this gang? Why doesn't anyone think about that? I should have been the leader when Shashidharan fell, and it was all spoiled with this damned madness. Tomorrow is the mad Musafir's last chance. Maybe I will perish. Otherwise? Whom should I shoot first? Getto? I also wonder why you betrayed Raul. Keep up the spirit till the end of the game. If it works out, we may confront each other in one round. But Satheeshan, this Musafir will aim for your head first. The gang doesn't require two madmen now.'

Bappu was tossing and turning in his bed. He was scared to sleep alone that night. Even though he had requested his daughter Laila to send her son to sleep next to him, she did not allow it, because his skin infection was getting particularly bad. He kept waking up from dreams of snakebites. He prayed and awaited the call for the Subahi namaz.

Lothar spent the entire night in front of the piano. In his mind he confessed to Dora, who was sleeping in the other room, remorseful for the truth behind the bad dream she had seen when she woke from her sleep ten or twelve years ago.

Dora, will you forgive Papa's sins? I am prepared now. Papa is ending with this, dear. Once this fire ends, don't wait for me or your Getto. I know you will be heartbroken when you hear about this. But I don't have any other solution to end this all. Your marriage should happen at the synagogue here. You should remember the twelve holy tribes of Israel and cleanse yourself twelve times. You should wear a long white gown, not those dark dresses I bought for you. Women will accompany you under the white sheet. They will encircle you and your groom and sing. Your face will blush and will shine like the Star of David.

He glanced at an old family photograph kept on top of the piano and drank as much as he could. The room filled with music until he lost consciousness and fell onto the keys of the piano.

Getto was still in the darkness of the antique shop. Musafir had informed him that a vehicle would be sent to pick him up in the morning. He became a patient listener for all the crying crickets around him. His memories kept bruising him like sharp weapons. To escape from them, he tried to immerse himself in beer, but his drunken father's stench choked him.

As usual, Satheeshan woke up from his sleep to the sound of the sixth bullet. He had prepared himself for the roulette. He was confident as ever yet confused as to who would point their gun at him and at whom he would point his gun. He decided that his first victim would either be Getto or Musafir, closed his eyes and prayed that his sleep wouldn't be broken now by another bullet.

Unni's wife picked up the insistently ringing phone and tried to wake him up. He was in his customary drunken slumber. He woke up and looked at his wife questioningly. She handed the phone over to him, mumbled, turned her back to him and went back to sleep. He yawned and spoke into the phone.

'What is it, Mustafa? Won't you let me sleep? Everything is okay. Why are you worried at this hour? There is no point worrying now. You should have thought about it when you chose to ride the elephant yourself instead of assigning a capable guy from your gang. I am meeting Getto tomorrow. Let me talk to him and see. All right then. Let's talk tomorrow.'

Unni covered his head with his blanket.

The city was asleep outside.

12

The Death Bet

Musafir had agreed to send a vehicle for Getto. But it was Unni who came to pick him up. After three days of hiding, when he went out in the daylight, he was welcomed with Unni's congratulations.

'You did it to that Raul, no? I really liked it. I had told Raul earlier that he shouldn't get into all this. But who listens to me? Unni is just a pimp, right? If I had pimped out, the gang also benefited from it. I have arranged women for police, advocates and magistrates to get you folks out of all kinds of criminal cases.'

Since Getto was absolutely sure that Unni wouldn't have done something like that for him ever, he smiled without making eye contact.

'Every goddamn thing is ending today. All the motherfuckers are in it together. Don't spoil it. You are entering the roulette for a different reason altogether. You should aim for Musafir or Satheeshan. If you are the least bit loyal to me, you must do it. I have fixed a deal with Pandam Mustafa.'

'What deal?'

'You must help Mustafa in this damned bet. He will help you out. You should forget everything about the past. You have had big conflicts, the two of you. But now, he doesn't hold any grudges.'

'I do not understand.'

'You must kill anyone of the other four you feel is aiming at Mustafa's head. Mustafa will take care of the one who comes for you.'

'What if Mustafa and I are the last men standing?'

'Isn't that the deal I talked about? If Mustafa and you remain, we will stop this game. Irrespective of the foreigner or the police controlling it from outside, it is not a big deal for Nambiar. Do you understand?'

'You are aware that nobody knows how things will work out. In an instant, things might topple over. Yet, since you have fixed the deal, I will act accordingly.'

'I was sure that you would listen to me. Let's see, then.'

They reached Unni's godown near Pathalam. Grusha's and Balakrishnan Nambiar's cars were already there. A little farther, there were Raul's old jeep and Lothar's bike. The godown was open, yet everyone was outside, waiting for Unni to arrive: Lothar was standing by his bike, and the rest of them were still inside their vehicles. Unni parked his car close to the godown and got out of the car.

'I told you guys not to park your vehicles outside like this. Are we going to let all the neighbours in?'

He returned to his car and drove it into the godown. The cars and jeep followed Unni. Everyone got out of their vehicles. Grusha was perplexed at the presence of Arumukhan as he climbed out of the jeep with Musafir and Satheeshan. Grusha did not recognize Mustafa until Bappu introduced the stranger with him. She couldn't believe that the infamous gang leader she had been hearing about was merely five and a half feet tall, skeletally built and well stubbled, with a pair of sad eyes. She realized that the city kept many other secrets for her to discover. She returned to the final arrangements for the death bet. Nambiar and Unni came up to her. Unni represented Grusha's company, and Nambiar was with the non-existent second company. Grusha looked at them and smiled.

The Star of David

It was a spacious godown with an asbestos roof. Unni used to keep the building materials there. In the middle of all the metal, wood, sacks of cement and other building tools, there was a tarpaulin sheet on the floor, demarcating the betting space. Unni had spread it himself to avoid having to clean up the space after the bloodshed. Grusha marked the design on the tarpaulin with a white marker. She then looked at everyone and started filling in their initials in the figure of the star. To mark Musafir apart from Mustafa, she gave Musafir an extra letter, S for

Sheikh. Grusha pointed towards the space each of them should occupy.

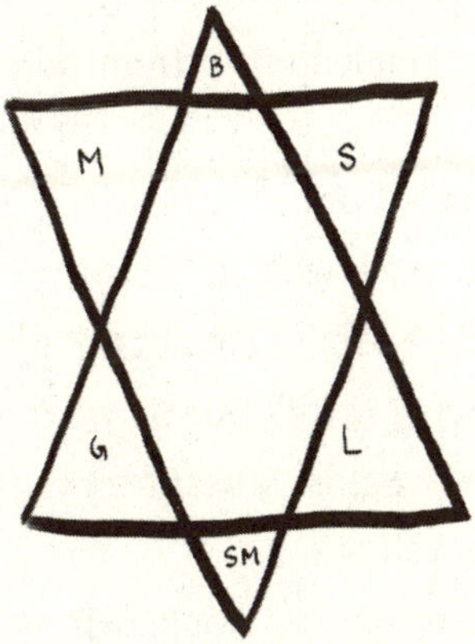

It was Lothar who first entered the corner of the Star of David earmarked for him, a triangular box with an L written in it. He kept his head held high, his hands close to his heart, and closed his eyes. After that, Bappu and Musafir stood opposite each other. Mustafa stood across from Lothar. In keeping with the secret deal between them, Getto occupied the box next to Pandam Mustafa. When Grusha entered the symbol with six guns in her hands and filled one bullet in each of them, Satheeshan's box was empty. He was standing next to Arumukhan outside the box, his head bent. Grusha doubtfully approached him and handed him a gun. Satheeshan kept his head down, failing to meet Grusha's eyes. When he realized that all eyes were on him, he handed over the gun to Arumukhan and declared, 'Arumukhan will play on my behalf.'

Satheeshan leaves the game

The gun fell from Arumukhan's hands. When Satheeshan picked it up and returned it to Arumukhan, Unni stopped him.

'Where are you headed off to from here? Stand in the box meant for you.'

Satheeshan pulled out a knife from his waistband and touched Unni's stomach with it.

'I have only declared that I am not taking part in this game. I am not afraid to die or to kill. Do you want to test it now?'

Unni walked backwards. Musafir moved out of his box and grabbed Satheeshan's neck.

'Great, you! I knew that you would behave like a bastard. Yet I didn't imagine that you would be this shameless. You go and hide in your mother's womb. A chieftain should fight with another of the same rank. I have heard about the story of Quixote who would send Sancho to fight the thugs they met on the way. Don't fight windmills. You come, if you dare, to fight real men.'

'This is a mere game of betting run by the companies, Bhai, not a matter of proving one's manhood. And the reason why I stepped back, consider it as a move when the king needs to hide for a while. It's called castling.'

Satheeshan pushed Musafir, who stumbled and fell to the ground. Satheeshan ran out, brandishing his knife. He started his car and reversed it out of the godown.

Unni, Nambiar and Bappu

Unni looked at Balakrishnan Nambiar and raised an eyebrow. Nambiar reached for the mobile phone in his pocket and walked towards a corner of the storage unit. He spoke to someone animatedly, gesticulating with his right hand as he spoke. He stopped talking in the middle and gestured towards Bappu to come closer. Bappu finished the conversation on the phone. He handed the mobile phone back to Nambiar and returned to his box. Nambiar stopped talking, went up to Unni and told him in a hushed voice, 'I have arranged it with Inspector Joy from the goon squad. They will finish Satheeshan today itself. We shouldn't meddle and mess it up. Do you understand?'

Grusha and Musafir

Grusha offered her hand to Musafir, who was still lying on the floor, and helped him up. He leaned against a table near the wall. She made sure that his hands were not shaking when she handed over the gun to him. From the coat pocket, she produced a new necktie and made Musafir wear it.

'Let this help Musafir the minister become the king.'

'Grusha, once this game is over, you should remember that the king, the bishop and the pawns will sleep in the same box.'

Musafir smirked. He didn't laugh loudly like Grusha's papa. He had no bodily resemblance to her papa. Yet when she looked at Musafir with his necktie, her eyes brimmed over... She remembered her papa. She closed her eyes in memory of those colourful ties she received as gifts. She prayed that this tie would not be stained with Musafir's blood. She cursed the moment when she had agreed to organize this roulette in return for money that would help her settle down in life. Like the God who asked Abraham not to kill his only son right before he was about to slash his throat, she hoped that the company would ask her to stop the game right before it began.

Arumukhan and Musafir

Arumukhan walked to his corner, then stepped closer to Musafir. He took Musafir's hands, along with the gun they held, pressed them to his chest and whimpered, 'I am not scared to die, Bhai. But Satheeshan didn't even ask me before he handed over this piece of metal to me. I need some time, Bhai. I will go out and come back soon. I want to see my mother one last time. I need to confess that it was me who killed my brother. I am not scared to go to any hell once I do that.'

'There is no time for all that, Arumukhan. If you leave in the middle, you are destined to die. The life of the one who left after putting the gun in your hand has been decided. There is no hope, my dear. If you want to meet your mother and confess, you have to get in and kill everyone. There is no going back otherwise. Do you even know how to use this gun?'

'A little bit...'

'Ah! That is enough.'

He guided Arumukhan to his corner and returned to his space.

Mustafa and Nambiar

'You are aware that this is a death bet,' Nambiar said to Mustafa. 'Can't take risks with it. On behalf of the company, I am betting on those who have the biggest chances to win. The company does not know vengeance or friendship. It only cares about success. The company felt that Satheeshan had a better chance of winning than you. But you just saw that Satheeshan believes in Arumukhan. I will be betting on Arumukhan in the first round, not you.'

'But that was not the deal between us, Nambiar! You told me that this is a chance to finish them all and only Bappu sir and I will have guns with bullets in it. Isn't that why we fixed the deal with Unni and that boy? This is a game with my life on the line. How the hell can you talk like this now? Why bet on Arumukhan now?'

'If you want to get out of it alive, you stand in the box, Mustafa. Otherwise, your fate will be the same as that of the one who has left the game.'

'In a betting shoot with six players, the name Arumukhan, which means the six-faced one, has special luck – right, Nambiar?' Mustafa said.

Nambiar laughed as if he had cracked a great joke. Mustafa suddenly remembered Uncle Narayan who used to wait for him on his way back from school.

Uncle Narayan's game

On his way back from the lower primary school, when all his friends left for their homes, Mustafa would walk with his friend Ravi on the mud road. Narayanettan (Uncle Narayan) would be sitting outside Thomas Mappila's shop with a beedi glowing between his lips. He would call them close. Even though they knew why he was calling them, for some reason, they could not help walking towards him. He would draw images of Ravi's and Mustafa's fathers in the dust and write their names down.

He would ask Mustafa to step on Ravi's father's head. Mustafa would do it.

'Didn't you see how he stepped on your father's head?' Narayan would tell Ravi.

'Yes, Uncle, but what can I do now?'

'If you are man enough, you will piss on his father's head.'

Ravi would obey Narayan. Mustafa and Ravi would start hitting each other. The buttons on their shirts would come off. They would roll in the mud, their shirts turning brown. They would return all the pencils and marbles they had lovingly shared while they were at school. Narayanettan would laugh. They would return to their homes, crying. Narayan would light another beedi.

'Why do you make them fight, Narayan?' Thomas Mappila would ask. But since he got more business from Narayan than from those kids who would occasionally buy sweets worth ten paise, he would not enquire further.

The next day, Ravi and Mustafa would have forgotten everything and would go to school, study and play. They would share pencils and marbles with each other. On their way back, Uncle Narayan would be waiting for them.

It was for him that Mustafa would smear some cow dung under his slippers. It was for him that Ravi refused to take a piss during the school recess.

Barring the deep tobacco stains on Narayanettan's teeth, Balakrishnan Nambiar reminded Mustafa of that laughter from his childhood.

The first round of the Russian roulette

Grusha announced that the roulette was about to begin. All six of them held their fingers to the triggers. The first shots were empty and ended up fooling everyone.

Mustafa had decided that he would aim at Arumukhan, on whom the company was betting instead of him. Yet, when Mustafa saw Arumukhan's anxious face, he felt pity towards his victim for the first time in his life. He couldn't pull the trigger. The anxious Arumukhan's first shot at Mustafa had ended in an empty sound. Yet he succeeded in shooting Mustafa in the forehead when he shot again. Arumukhan had aimed for his chest. Since Arumukhan's gun was now empty, Grusha guessed that the others would aim at all those people with loaded guns now. She calculated, therefore, that Arumukhan had already won that round.

According to the deal with Unni, Getto aimed at Arumukhan, who was trying to shoot Mustafa. Both Musafir and Lothar had their focus on Getto. Mustafa had already fallen to Arumukhan's gun. When Mustafa fell, Getto forgot his deal and aimed at Sheikh Musafir. Both Getto's and Musafir's attempts were futile, but Lothar's gun had a shot. Getto got shot in the chest.

Both Lothar's gun aiming at Getto and Bappu's gun aiming at Lothar fired at the same time. Lothar was hit near his left eyebrow. While he writhed in one corner of the Star of David, his long fingers moved as if they were playing on the piano keys.

Bappu had assumed that the gun he held had already been loaded with bullets, with the last one being filled by Grusha before the players. That was the deal he had made with Nambiar. He was to shoot at all the others except Mustafa. When he realized he did not have a fully loaded revolver and his chances were being wasted, shadows of doubt spread across his face.

Sheikh Musafir tried to shoot Getto down thrice, but luck did not favour him. When Lothar's bullet shot Getto down, Musafir wondered whom to aim at now. He looked at Bappu, who carried an empty gun and wore a confused look. Musafir pulled his trigger on Bappu, the perjurer in the courtroom during the trial of Rajan. Like the court, his gun also betrayed him.

Musafir aimed again at Bappu's khaki uniform, the same Bappu who had crushed Albert's muscles on the table at the station with a coconut. Bappu fell down.

Musafir kept blinking as he looked at the blood spreading on the floor. When the first round of the roulette ended, only Arumukhan and Musafir were left. Musafir looked at the distressed Arumukhan's face and smirked. Grusha took the guns from both their hands, filled one bullet each and returned it to them. Weeping, Arumukhan kissed the locket of Velmurugan that hung around his neck and walked towards Musafir.

'Bhai, how can I?'

'You guys, go to your box!' Musafir screamed, his gun aimed at Arumukhan.

Arumukhan returned to his space, trembling with fear.

Arumukhan had won the first round. But Unni had noticed how his hands were not steady and how his aim had missed. In the second round, he bet on the mad Musafir.

Balakrishnan Nambiar, however, was not ready to change his bet from Arumukhan. Arumukhan with shaky hands was still better than a mad Musafir.

Neither Musafir nor Arumukhan knew who had placed their bets on them.

Grusha announced the commencement of the second round of the roulette.

The second round

As he lay in his corner, struggling for his life, Getto had seen how Musafir kept blinking. That was a sign that Musafir was about to go over the line of reason. The dead bodies that fell around him and the blood that was spreading on the tarpaulin were driving him over the edge. He had also noticed how he addressed Arumukhan as 'you guys'. Musafir had once confessed to Getto that when in the throes of his madness, he often saw Arumukhan as the twin Arumukhans, with the dead one repeating his brother's actions. Once when Arumukhan visited him at the mental hospital at Kumudagiri, Musafir asked Arumukhan if 'you guys' were well.

Even as he lay dying, a comical curiosity filled Getto. Of the two Arumukhans Musafir was seeing, which one would he try to shoot? Would the bullet hit the dead Arumukhan or the living one? Musafir functioned like an oddly timed Shakespearean sonnet. It was his gun that fired first. The bullet missed its target and hit the wall. It was possible that Musafir had been aiming at the younger one. The scared Arumukhan closed his eyes and pulled his trigger over and over.

Balakrishnan Nambiar perhaps knew that the scared and shivering Arumukhan would not be enough to kill Musafir. He touched Unni's shoulder. Unni took out a gun he had hidden behind him and pointed it at Musafir. Before Grusha could scream 'no', Musafir had already got shot from the back. His gun dropped from his hands.

In shock from the sound of that shot, Arumukhan closed his eyes as he pulled the trigger again. Before he realized that Musafir, with his empty gun, was not dangerous and perhaps he could bring an end to the roulette, he had already fired his gun. Musafir got shot a second time, near his heart.

Musafir fell to the ground, clutching the bullet wound in his chest. Getto expected him to utter the iconic line 'Et tu, Brute?' from the play *Julius Caesar*. Since Musafir was a fan of Shakespeare, it was not difficult to imagine a death scene like that for him. As he awaited his own death, Getto expected Musafir to say that to Unni. Yet, undoing all his hopes, Musafir died with the name of God on his lips.

'Traitor Musafir' – those were Getto's last words.

In another location, Satheeshan was becoming an invisible participant in the roulette. Two police jeeps and three motorbikes that belonged to the anti-goon squad encircled Satheeshan. One among them was the driver of Grusha's car. When he realized that he could not escape from this trap, he turned off the car engine and closed his eyes, his head on the steering wheel.

By the time the squad vehicles left, there were six bullets in Satheeshan's body. He didn't wake up even at the sixth bullet. There was an empty gun in his hand, like an accompaniment from his dream.

Grusha returned in Unni's car. Unni was driving very slowly, following Balakrishnan Nambiar's car that went ahead of them. When they reached the highway, he turned his CD player on. Aviyal, an indie rock band, came on with an ear-shattering guitar riff. Unni tapped on the steering wheel to the tune of the song. Grusha closed her eyes.

Arumukhan stumbled out of the godown into a silent street filled with blinding sunlight.

13

Thereafter

Aaby was in bed with a fever when he received the telegram carrying the news of Lothar's death. Isaac read it out to him. Aaby jolted upright and sat restlessly awhile, with his eyes closed and fingers crisscrossed over his nose.

'I need to reach Kochi immediately. Get a ticket.'

'But you are in no position to–'

'Isaac, do as I say.'

Knowing how his father had not changed one bit even in his declining years, Isaac immediately started contacting one travel agency after another.

'There are no tickets for today on flights or trains. Can be done for tomorrow. One travel agency has a single ticket available. But how will you go alone in this condition?'

'Book that one, Isaac,' Aaby said, cutting Isaac short.

After a couple of days of wandering in an alcoholic daze, Arumukhan had reached Ernakulam South railway station. He did not know where to go next. He found an unoccupied bench on the platform. He lay down on it, one hand resting on his knee, the other, bruised, folded and turned into a makeshift pillow. His arm held the scent of sweat, reminding him of his father's deathbed and the whiff of sweat on his father's chest. He feared his death and looked up with a deep sigh.

When Aaby got off his train, Arumukhan was waiting for a train on the opposite platform, trying to get as far away from that city as he could.

At the hotel, Grusha could not remember how long she stood under the shower. A shiver spread across her body and brought her back from the recurring memories that reeked of death. She patted her hair and stomach dry and walked to the bedroom, letting her dripping naked body relax on the bed. She turned off the music on her laptop and opened her inbox. The first email was from Carl. Grusha wondered if she would change her decision if she started to read that email. Before she read Carl's email, she typed out a brief letter of resignation and sent it to the manager of her company, including a copy to Carl. After that, she opened his email.

Dear Grusha,

I guess the Russian roulette is over. The company managers and the CEO will be eagerly awaiting your report now.

I can guess what you are feeling about me. Nothing can save me – not the porn movies I like to watch or the prostitutes with their black pantyhose or the gambling tiles at Vegas. Since I have told you this much, if you assume this to be a confessional letter, you are mistaken again. I am going to tell you about some really scary escapades I have had in my life.

The baseless fears in my life started from a book. When I was eight years old and had caught chickenpox, my grandfather gave me a book to kill time. It was an old copy of Oliver Twist. *It might have been older than my grandfather. Since I had boils all over, I couldn't read for long. My grandfather read the book to me. While he was reading, he used to imitate the different characters. It was almost as if my grandfather's face was a storybook in 3D. I was most afraid of Fagin. I lost my sleep, imagining his long nose, grey hair, stained teeth, wrinkly skin and his faded old coat. Even after my chickenpox was cured, my fears about Fagin stayed. I started to fear the darkness. I started hating the dark corridor I had to pass through to reach my room after dinner.*

It was not his ugly appearance that scared me. I feared that one day, while walking through that dark corridor, Fagin might kidnap me. It would be all right if he was kidnapping me to kill me. But what I feared was that he would take me to a dark underworld space where he would hurt me and threaten me and teach me to pick pockets. I would spend some time as a pickpocket and a thief before I graduated to a street thug. I would lead my life spreading fear all over the city. Fagin would give me a life I could never bear to live. In his world, I would have roamed around the city with weapons, searching for my opponents.

Grusha, in that roulette, you let a lot of Fagins die. They were the ones who would kidnap kids and transform them into pickpockets and thugs. You don't need to feel guilty at all. If you think about it, what if it was all a dream? Once you return, after your long flight, this will be as distant as a dream. Such vague memories. Perhaps you might need some help to tame those memories.

Did I tell you about a white bird that I saw in the winter? It was the day before Thanksgiving, three years back. All of a sudden, we received safety warnings about a snowstorm. There was an announcement to evacuate the office immediately. Even though the others left immediately, since I had some urgent work to finish, I had stayed back and was the last person to leave. By that time, there was a heavy blizzard. I had parked my car outside the office. While I was walking towards the car, I saw something interesting. A little bird was sitting on the rearview mirror, a bird whiter than the snow. It was trying to fly off. Yet, in the snowstorm, it couldn't lift itself and would come back and sit on my mirror. By the time I reached my car, it had tried this five times. It was shivering in the cold. I tried to catch hold of it, but it resisted, injuring my hands and attempting to fly away. I was sure that it would die in the blizzard. Even though I had started my car engine, I was stuck there, thinking about what to do about the bird.

Since I had the spectre of Fagin in my mind, I started fearing whether he had come in the guise of this bird. A police car came to rescue me and the bird. A policeman approached my car and asked me why I was not moving my car. I pointed at the bird sitting on the rearview mirror and lied that I was planning how to save that one. In reality, I was the one who was searching for help to escape. From the shapeshifter Fagin...from the bad weather... The policeman smiled at me, looked at the bird and whistled. The bird magically went and sat on his arm like it was his pet. He went back to his vehicle with the bird and gestured at me to leave the place. I drove my car fast, as if I was escaping from that place.

When I returned to office and narrated the story to all of you, even I had forgotten most of the details. Nobody had seen such a white bird in those parts of the town in winter. People made fun of me, as if I was making it all up. Even I started to doubt whether the bird was real. I firmly believed that I had imagined it.

Grusha, while I am typing this, I cannot believe that it was just my imagination. Yet I suspect that it was. It is as unbelievable as a Fagin out there to get me. Yes, I am coming back to Fagin. The same Charles Dickens who wrote Oliver Twist, *planting the most irrational fears about Fagin, also taught me how I must correct myself and escape. Dickens had introduced Fagin as a representative of the Jewish community when he first wrote the book. In many places, he had even used the term Old Jew. Yet, in the later editions, Dickens made some changes. It was because of a business relationship. Dickens had sold his London home to a Jewish moneylender. The Jew had kept such cordial relations with him during the business deal that it surprised Dickens. He was corrected of his own perceptions of the greedy Jew. He erased the anti-Semitic remarks from the story on the request of that moneylender's wife. In his later writings, he also created many good Jewish characters.*

Grusha, can you guess how a small business deal can transform people? If that is so, how big will the changes be between big companies, marketplaces and businesses? These companies are old Fagins. Since we have no other resort, we might have to learn to pick pockets and enter the streets. I have received my transfer order. In another two weeks, I will be there in Kochi. You should convey my love to our unborn child.

With love,
C.W.

Grusha sighed in relief that she had already sent the resignation letter before reading Carl's email. She wanted to ask Carl why they had left Arumukhan alone after their death bet. She realized that she could not handle the responses and the secrets in those responses. She emailed Uncle Alan the details of preparations for her trip with her mother, and before she shut her laptop down, she searched for the folder where she kept her father's pictures cut out from old family photos. She realized that it was more difficult to fix him back into the photographs than it was to remove him. By the time she had successfully reinserted her father into her family pictures, the father without dragon tattoos or guns, her eyes were aching.

She closed her eyes slowly and ducked into her childhood. She could smell her mother's cooking. Since the picture was finished, her father's room did not have those Chinese dragons. Her papa was also not visible. He must be hiding behind a door to startle her after placing the gift tie on the tabletop. Grusha opened her eyes and without a second thought deleted the picture she had spent hours to fix. She closed the laptop, put it aside, closed her eyes again and caressed her bare belly. She wanted to say something aloud, but an ineffable sadness choked her voice.

Author's Acknowledgements

I would like to express my heartfelt gratitude to the following individuals who helped me bring this novel to life:

To Kanishka Gupta, for believing in my work and advocating for it to find its place in the publishing world.

To Padmini Smetacek and Shantanu Ray Chaudhuri, for their meticulous editing and insightful feedback in bringing out the best in my writing.

To Sini Sunil, Swarnima Narayan, and Abhivyakti Singh from Hachette India, for their vision, support and guidance in driving this project from conception to completion.

And last but not least, to Prabha Zacharias, for the skilful translation that has made this novel accessible to a wider audience.

Translator's Acknowledgements

My heartfelt gratitude to the author V.M. Devadas for trusting me with this work.